Dear Reader,

Looking back over the years, I find it hard to realise that twenty-six of them have gone by since I wrote my first book—*Sister Peters in Amsterdam*. It wasn't until I started writing about her that I found that once I had started writing, nothing was going to make me stop—and at that time I had no intention of sending it to a publisher. It was my daughter who urged me to try my luck.

I shall never forget the thrill of having my first book accepted. A thrill I still get each time a new story is accepted. Writing to me is such a pleasure, and seeing a story unfolding on my old typewriter is like watching a film and wondering how it will end. Happily of course.

To have so many of my books re-published is such a delightful thing to happen and I can only hope that those who read them will share my pleasure in seeing them on the bookshelves again. . .and enjoy reading them.

Back by Popular Demand

A collector's edition of favourite titles from one of the world's best-loved romance authors. Mills & Boon are proud to bring back these sought after titles and present them as one cherished collection.

BETTY NEELS: COLLECTOR'S EDITION

GRASP A NETTLE

BY
BETTY NEELS

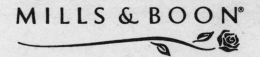

MILLS & BOON®

*All the characters in this book have no existence outside the imagina-
tion of the author, and have no relation whatsoever to anyone bearing
the same name or names. They are not even distantly inspired by any
individual known or unknown to the author, and all the incidents are
pure invention.*

*First published in Great Britain 1977 by Mills & Boon Limited
This edition 1999
Harlequin Mills & Boon Limited,
Eton House, 18-24 Paradise Road, Richmond, Surrey TW9 1SR*

© Betty Neels 1977

ISBN 0 263 80701 0

*Set in Times Roman 11 on 12½ pt by
Rowland Phototypesetting Limited
Bury St Edmunds, Suffolk*

73-9908-46582

*Made and printed in Great Britain by
Caledonian International Book Manufacturing Ltd, Glasgow*

Tender-handed stroke a nettle
And it stings you for your pains;
Grasp it like a man of mettle
And it soft as silk remains.

AARON HILL

CHAPTER ONE

THE winding stone staircase in the corner tower was gloomy excepting for the regular patches of sunlight from the narrow slit windows set at intervals in its thick stone walls, but the girl running up the worn steps thought nothing of the gloom; she was well accustomed to it. She paused now, half way up, to peer out of one of the windows, craning her neck to look along the back drive to Dimworth House. It was almost two o'clock and the first of the visitors were already driving slowly down the narrow, ill-made lane which ran for a mile or more on its way from the main road.

The girl turned her bright coppery head to look down at the wide gravel path bordered by lawns and herbaceous borders, to where, beyond the open gate at its far end, the field used as a car park was waiting, empty, for the cars to fill it. It promised to be a good day in terms of entrance fees; although Dimworth House was one of the smaller stately homes open to the public, it was doing quite nicely, although it meant hard work for the family, and indeed, for everyone connected with the estate. The girl left the window presently, ran up the last curve of the narrow staircase, and pushed open the arched door at its top. It led to a small circular lobby, panelled and empty of furniture. She crossed this, opened the door in the opposite wall and entered a short, carpeted corridor, the walls hung with paintings and with a number of doors in its inner wall. There was a rather fine staircase half way along it, leading to the floor below, and a long latticed window lighting the whole, although not very adequately. The girl hurried along with the air of one familiar with her surroundings and knocked on the end door, and on being bidden to enter, did so.

The apartment was large, low-ceilinged and panelled, furnished with a variety of antique furniture, presided over by an enormous fourposter bed, and was occupied by a very upright elderly lady, sitting at a writing table under the window. She looked up as the girl went in, said: 'Ah, Jenny,' in a commanding voice and laid down her pen.

The girl had a charming voice. 'I found Baxter, he was in the water garden. He'll do the tickets— he's putting on a tie and washing his hands, and Mrs Thorpe says she'll take over from me at four o'clock.' She glanced at the carriage clock on the desk. 'I'd better get down to the hall, the cars are starting to arrive, Aunt Bess.'

'Dear child!' declared her aunt. 'I can't imagine what we shall do when you go back to that hospital tomorrow.' She coughed. 'I'm afraid it hasn't been much of a holiday for you.'

Her niece smiled. 'I've loved it,' she assured her relation, 'it's been a nice change from theatre, you know. I'm sorry I can't stay here for the rest of the summer.' She had wandered to the window to look out, and the sunshine shone on her bright hair, tied back loosely, and her pretty face, with its hazel eyes, thickly fringed, little tiptilted nose and generous mouth. She was of average height, nicely rounded and gloriously tanned with a sprinkling of freckles across the bridge of her nose.

The Hon. Miss Elizabeth Creed, her mother's sister and a lady of forceful disposition, smiled as she watched her, for she was the only one, bar her great-nephew, for whom she had any affection. Jenny had never allowed her aunt's caustic tongue to worry her; and although she had been left an orphan at an early age, she had never once asked for money or help of any kind. True, she had a quite adequate income of her own from the trust set up for her by her parents, as well as her salary, but that was chickenfeed compared to the annual revenues enjoyed by her aunt and the very generous allowance given to her dead cousin's widow and small son, Oliver, who would one day inherit Dimworth and a handsome fortune with it. In the meantime, however, his mother chose to live in Scotland with her parents, and the house was run by his great-aunt until such time as he was considered old enough to do this for himself.

Jenny, who spent her holidays with Aunt Bess, thought it a great pity that the little boy didn't live at Dimworth, for it was a beautiful place and peaceful, and her cousin, who had died in an air crash a year or so after his marriage, had loved it dearly and would surely have wanted his son to have been brought up there, but Margaret, his widow, had never liked it over-much; she came to stay from time to time, but always made it clear to the rest of the family that she was glad to go again. She would be coming within a few days, bringing the little boy with her, and Jenny had every intention of spending all her days off at Dimworth while he was there, for the two of them were the greatest of friends, and Margaret, beautiful and languid and not particularly maternal, soon tired of his youthful high spirits.

Jenny, leaving her aunt to her writing, skipped down the staircase, crossed the landing below and opened a carved oak door on to a richly furnished sitting room overlooking the front of the house, and through which she threaded her way without loss of time, to go through a small, very old arched door cut into one of its walls. It led to another staircase, a very small one, down which she trod, to open an even smaller door at the bottom opening directly into the entrance hall of the house. There was a large table set in the centre of this vast area, laid out neatly with brochures, postcards, small souvenirs, pots of homemade jam and the like, and she made for the chair at its centre and took her seat just as the first of the visitors poked enquiring heads through the open doors.

The next two hours went fast. Jenny had been right, there were a good number of visitors, and when she had done her stint in the hall and Mrs Thorpe, the vicar's wife, very correctly dressed in her best summer two-piece and a good hat, had taken over from her, she went across to the old stables, converted into a tea-room, and found that it was nicely filled with family parties, tucking into their cream teas. Florrie, the indispensable housekeeper, and her niece Felicity were managing very well between them, so Jenny made her way back to the house, to enter it by a small door at the side, which led via a back hall into the last of the chain of rooms on view to the public—the dining room, sombre and panelled in oak, its refectory table and massive oak chairs protected by crimson ropes, and the silver goblets and plates on the great table protected by a burglar alarm which no one could see; they gleamed richly against the dark wood.

There were a dozen people there, standing about staring at the treasures around them, gazing without a great deal of interest at the dark oil paintings on the walls—family portraits, and not very colourful ones, although if any of them had studied them closely they would have noticed that most of them portrayed a variety of people with coppery hair, just like Jenny's.

The next room leading from the dining room was crowded, as it usually was; it was a small apartment, its walls lined with bookshelves, and arranged on a number of small tables was the collection of dolls which Aunt Bess had occupied herself in collecting over the years. This small room led in its turn to the blue drawing room, lofty and rather grand with its ornate ceiling and silk-hung walls, and furnished with gilded chairs and tables and a magnificent harpsichord. The little anteroom leading from it was far more to Jenny's taste; panelled in pinewood and rather crowded with Regency furniture, surprisingly comfortable to sit on. The family sometimes used the room in the summer, but once the evenings became chilly it was more prudent to stay in the private wing, for a small staircase led from the anteroom, up and down which the wind whistled, leaving anyone silly enough to sit there chilled to the bone.

Jenny didn't pause, but went up the staircase to cast an eye over the three bedrooms on view. No one had used them for very many years now. Their fourposters were magnificent, the heavy tables and mirrors and chests worth a fortune, but they held little comfort. There were quite a few people here too; she mingled with them, answering a few questions and cautioning people that the stone staircase leading down to the hall was worn in places and needed care before slipping away again, this time to go through yet another of the small doors which peppered the house, into the private wing. It was cosy here, with thick carpets underfoot, damask curtains at the mullioned windows, and a nicely balanced mixture of period furniture. Jenny's room was down a narrow passage, a roomy apartment with a small sitting room adjoining it and a bathroom on its other side. She had always occupied it, ever since, as a small child, she had spent her holidays at Dimworth.

She went straight to the wall closet now, gathered an armful of clothes and began to pack with speed and neatness. She intended leaving early the next morning, driving herself in the Morgan two-seater which Aunt Bess had given her for her twenty-first birthday; she had had it for four years now, and drove it superbly, making light of the journey to and from London, a journey she made at least twice a month. She would have liked to have spent all her days off at Dimworth, but she had a great many friends in and around the hospital—besides, Toby Blake, the elder son of Aunt Bess's nearest neighbour, might feel encouraged to propose to her yet again if she went down there too often. She frowned now, thinking about him; she supposed that sooner or later she would marry him, not because she was in love with him, but because they had known each other for such a long time and everyone expected them to. She was aware that this was no reason to accept him, but he did persist. 'Water wearing out a stone,' she commented to the room around her as she shut her case, took a cursory look in the mirror and went to find her aunt.

Tea was a meal which, on the days when the house was open to the public, was a moveable feast in the small sitting room on the ground floor. Anyone who had the time had a cup, and old Grimshaw, the butler, made it his business to tread to and fro with fresh tea as it was required. He was on the lookout now for Jenny and as she gained the lower hall, said in his fatherly fashion: 'I'll bring tea at once, Miss Jenny,' and disappeared through the baize door beside the stairs, kitchenwards.

Jer.ny called after him: 'Oh, good,' and added: 'I'm famished, Grimshaw,' as she opened the door and went in. Her aunt was sitting by the open window, her tea on the sofa table beside her chair.

'I must have an aspirin,' she declared in a voice so unlike her own that Jenny hurried over to her. 'I have the most terrible headache.'

'You've been working too hard, Aunt Bess. I'll get them. . .in your room?'

Her aunt nodded and she sped away to return at the same time as Grimshaw with the teapot. She poured her aunt another cup and shook out two tablets and offered them to her. 'Do you often get headaches?' she enquired, casting a professional eye over the elderly white strained face.

'I've never had a headache in my life before,' observed Miss Creed sharply, 'only these last few weeks. . .'

'And aspirins help?'

'Not really.' She was sitting back in her chair, her eyes closed.

'Then let's get Doctor Toms to see you.'

Miss Creed opened her eyes and sat up very straight. 'We will do no such thing, Janet. I'm never ill. You will oblige me by not referring to it again.'

'Well,' said Jenny reasonably, 'if you have any more headaches like this one, I shall certainly refer to it. Probably you need stronger glasses.'

Her aunt turned her head to look at her as she stood at the table, pouring herself her tea. 'H'm— perhaps that's it. You're a sensible girl, Jenny.'

Jenny smiled at her; her aunt always called her Janet when she was vexed, now she was Jenny again. They began to talk of other things and her aunt's indisposition wasn't mentioned again that day. Only the next morning when she went along to her aunt's room to wish her goodbye did that formidable lady declare: 'If ever I should be ill,

Jenny, I should wish you to nurse me.' And Jenny,
noting uneasily the pallor of the face on the pillows, said hearteningly: 'You're never ill, my
dear, but if ever you are, yes, I'll look after you—
you know that.' She bent to kiss the elderly cheek.
'You've been father and mother to me for almost
all of my life, and very nice parents you've been,
too.' She went to the door. 'I'll be back in ten
days' time and I'll telephone late this evening
unless anything crops up.'

London at the end of summer was crowded,
hot, and smelled of petrol. Jenny wrinkled her
nose as she drove across its heart and into the
East End. When she had started her training as a
nurse, her family, particularly Margaret, had been
annoyed at her choice of hospital. With all the
teaching hospitals to choose from, she had elected
to apply to Queen's, large and old-fashioned and
set squarely in the East End; not the type of place
which, since she had insisted on taking up
nursing, a Creed or a Wren should choose. But
Jenny had had her own way, for despite her pretty
face she was a determined girl with a quite nasty
temper to go with her hair, and she had done her
three years general training, followed it with a
midwifery certificate and now held the post of
Junior Theatre Sister. Her family still smiled tol-
erantly at the idea of her having a career, thinking
no doubt of Toby Blake waiting in the wings, as
it were; sure that very soon now she would realise

that to be married to him would be pleasant and suitable and what was expected of her. But Jenny had other ideas, although she wasn't able to clarify them, even to herself. There would be someone in the world meant for her; she had been sure of that ever since she was a little girl, and although there was no sign of him yet, she was still quite certain that one day she would come face to face with him, and he would feel just as she did—and in the meantime she intended to make a success of her job.

Queen's looked grey and forbidding from the outside, and indeed, on the inside as well, but she no longer noticed the large draughty entrance hall, nor the long dark passages leading from it. She plunged into them after a cheerful exchange of greetings with the head porter, and presently went through a door, painted a dismal brown, across a courtyard overlooked by most of the hospital's wards, and into the Nurses' Home, an old-fashioned building which had been altered and up-dated whenever there had been any money to spare, so that it presented a hotchpotch of styles and building materials. But inside it was fairly up-to-date, with the warden's office just inside the door and a wide staircase beside the two lifts. Jenny wished the warden, Miss Mellow—who wasn't in the least mellow—a staid good morning, for it had barely struck noon, and started up the stairs, taking the handful of letters Miss

Mellow had wordlessly handed her with her.

Three of them were from Toby; he was a great letter writer; his handwriting small and neat and unmistakable. Jenny sighed as she saw it and glanced at the others; from friends who had married and left hospital, inviting her severally for a weekend, to dinner, and to meet for coffee one day soon. She read them as she wandered upstairs, for she wasn't on duty until the following morning and she had plenty of time to unpack and get her uniform ready. But Toby's letters she didn't open, not until she had gained her room on the third floor, put her case down, kicked off her shoes and curled up on her bed.

There was nothing to say in any of them which she didn't know already, and why he had to write on three successive days to point out the advantages of marrying him was a mystery—besides, she had seen him only four days ago, and when, as usual, he had asked her to marry him she had said quite definitely, with the frankness of an old friend, that it just wouldn't work. She put the letters down after a while and went along to the pantry to make a pot of tea. Clare Brook was there, putting on the kettle, having had a free morning from Women's Surgical, and she greeted Jenny with a cheerful 'Hullo,' and went on in mock dismay: 'You're on call tonight, ducky. Old Hickory (Miss Dock, the Theatre Superintendent) is off with toothache, Maureen's got days off and

Celia being Celia and left in charge doesn't feel she should.' She raised her eyes to the ceiling. 'Our Celia is getting too big for her boots, just because Mr Wilson likes the way she hands him the instruments... So there you are, Jenny Wren, and for sure there'll be a massive RTA and you'll be up all night.'

Jenny spooned tea into the pot. 'Well, I've been away for two weeks,' she observed, 'so I suppose it's fair enough, though it's beastly to come back to.'

Clare eyed her with interest. 'Had a good time at that ancestral hall of yours? Seven-course dinners every evening, I suppose, and a dress for each one...' She spoke without rancour; everyone liked Jenny and nobody grudged her her exalted background. 'Not engaged to that Toby of yours yet?'

Jenny spooned sugar into their mugs and reached for the biscuit tin. 'No—it's silly of me, but I just know we wouldn't suit. Well, what I mean is...' she frowned, wishing to make herself clear: 'We've known each other simply years and years, and there's no...no...'

'Spice? I know what you mean—you're so used to each other you don't even quarrel.'

'He has a very even temper...'

'Huh—so there's nothing for you to sharpen your bad moods on, is there? You need someone with a temper as fine as yours, my dear, without an ounce of meekness in him, to give as good as he gets.'

'It doesn't sound very comfortable,' protested Jenny.

'Who wants to be comfortable? Chris and I fight quite a bit, you know, and we're only engaged. Heaven knows what it'll be like when we marry, but it'll never be dull.' Clare handed her mug over for more tea. 'Which reminds me, I saw the sweetest wedding dress the other day. . .'

The pair of them became absorbed in the interesting world of fashion.

Jenny had to get up during the night, not for the massive RTA which Clare had prophesied, but for a little boy who had fallen out of his bedroom window to the pavement below; it took hours to patch him up and his chance of survival was so slim as to be almost non-existent. Jenny, going back to bed at three o'clock in the morning, lay awake worrying about him for another hour, so that when she got down to breakfast at half past seven her pretty face was pale and tired, but the news that the child was still alive cheered her up and she ate her breakfast with a fair appetite, wishing, as she always did, that she was back at Dimworth, having her breakfast in the little sitting room overlooking the water garden, with Aunt Bess sitting opposite, reading indignant pieces from the newspaper and calling everybody, impartially, a fool.

There was a heavy list for the morning and Celia Drake, assuming the mantle Miss Dock had temporarily laid down, was at her most trying; if the morning's work was to run smoothly, then both of them would have to work, sharing the cases. But Celia, topheavy with importance, had elected to take the easiest of the list and leave the long-drawn-out ones to Jenny, which meant that Jenny wasn't going to get off duty punctually; the list would drag on until after dinner and there would be a wild scramble to get the afternoon list started on time, and although it wasn't a long one, Jenny guessed who would be scrubbing for it.

She eyed the cases she was expected to deal with and frowned heavily, her lovely hazel eyes dark with temper, while her coppery hair seemed to glow. Celia had retired to the office, probably to sit at the desk and dream of the day when she would—perhaps—be Theatre Superintendent. Jenny poked her indignant head round the door and gave her a fuming look.

'Come on out and do your share, Celia,' she invited waspishly. 'You're not in Old Hickory's shoes yet, you know. We'll share this list, half and half, and if you don't like the idea, I'll drop everything and go off sick.'

Celia might hand the instruments with *éclat*, but her wits weren't all that quick. 'Go off sick?' she wanted to know. 'But you're not. . .'

Jenny nodded her bright head vigorously. 'Oh, but I am—sick of you. What's it to be?'

'Oh, all right,' declared Celia peevishly, and added nastily: 'I don't see why you should have it all your own way just because there's a baron in your family.'

'I've got his red hair,' Jenny pointed out, 'and his nasty temper.'

The day was long and hot and tiring; the cases ran over their times and small complications cropped up which no one could have foreseen; consequently by the end of the morning's list the surgeons were a little edgy, the housemen ravenous because they hadn't had a coffee break, and the nurses' dinnertime hopelessly late. Jenny saw the last case out of theatre, sent as many nurses as she could spare to their meal, drank a hasty cup of tea with the surgeons, and aided by the one nurse she had kept back, started on getting ready for the afternoon's list. Her staff nurse would be back in time to scrub for the first case, and the list was a straightforward one. She might even have time to eat a sandwich and have another cup of tea.

She did, while Staff took the cholestectomy, and as she made her hasty meal she wrote up the books and then put the rest of the paper work on one side before going into theatre to scrub for the rest of the list. They were finished by five o'clock, but there was still the desk work to get through.

Celia, with a much shorter list, had already gone off duty, and Jenny sat in her office, writing swiftly in her rather wild handwriting, one ear cocked at the various familiar sounds coming from the theatre unit. She had two nurses on now, and a part-time staff nurse coming on duty at six o'clock. With luck, she would be finished by then.

It was too late to go out by the time she got off duty, and besides, she was tired; she took a bath and put on slacks and blouse and went to her supper, then sat around in the Sisters' sitting room, talking over the inevitable cups of tea. She was on the point of going to her bed when Miss Mellow arrived to request her presence in the telephone box in the hall. She spoke grudgingly, for she disliked what she called running messages, and she disliked Jenny too, partly because she was a pretty girl and partly because she came from that class of society which Miss Mellow always referred to as They. Jenny, who didn't like Miss Mellow either but had the good manners not to show it, thanked her nicely and went without haste to the callbox; it would be Toby—she sighed as she picked up the receiver. But it wasn't Toby, it was Doctor Toms. His voice, as mild as usual but carrying a note of urgency, surprised her. He wanted her at Dimworth. Miss Creed was ill and was asking for her.

'Now?' asked Jenny.

'Yes, my dear. Your aunt is very insistent that you should come.'

'Those headaches!' she exclaimed, remembering.

'Very severe—I want her to be seen by a specialist, but she says she'll do nothing until you're here.'

'Blackouts?' asked Jenny.

'Two today—probably she's had others and has told no one.'

Jenny glanced at her watch. 'I'll come at once, just as soon as I can fix things here. Will you ask someone to leave the side door open please—I ought to be with you by two o'clock.'

'Good girl! I shall be here, Jenny, with your aunt.'

She rang off and raced out of the home and across to the hospital, Night Super would be on duty by now, but heaven knew how far she had got with her first round. Jenny took five precious minutes tracking her down, and ran her to earth at last in the children's ward, where she held a hurried whispered conversation with her. Mrs Dent was a sensible, kindly woman, who listened without interruption before saying that of course Jenny must go at once and she would see that all the right people were informed in the morning. She even asked Jenny if she had enough money and if she would like a hot drink before she went. Jenny said yes, thank you and no, thank you with real gratitude and went back through the quiet hospital to her room, to fling clothes into a bag, explain her sudden departure to Celia, and go to the car park behind the hospital where she kept the Morgan.

She thanked heaven silently as she turned into the almost empty street that she had filled up on her way into London; there was enough petrol in the tank to get her to Dimworth. It was getting on for eleven o'clock by now, but once clear of London she made good time on the motorway; the clock tower bell chimed two as she stopped the car outside the private wing of the house. There was a light showing through the transom over the side door, and when she turned the handle, it opened silently under her hand. She stopped to bolt it before running up the stairs and along the corridor to her aunt's room. The door was slightly open and when she pushed it wide she saw Doctor Toms there, sitting in an armchair by the bed. He got up when she went in, but before he could speak Aunt Bess, her commanding voice a mcrc thread of hesitating sound, spoke.

'Jenny! You made good time. Don't let Doctor Toms frighten you. All this fuss about a headache. . .'

Jenny went to the bed and looked down at her aunt. She didn't like what she saw. Her aunt had looked off colour when she had left only two days earlier, but now she looked ill; her breathing was bad, her colour ghastly, and the pupils of her pale blue eyes were fixed and small. All the same, the lady of the house hadn't lost any of her fire. She spoke now in a snappy voice. 'Doctor Toms wants me to be seen by some puffed-up professor or other——he happens to be staying with him. I won't hear of it.'

'Why not, Aunt Bess?'

'He's a foreigner for a start,' Miss Creed's voice was slightly slurred. 'He's bound to be too big for his boots and make something out of nothing and then charge me a small fortune.'

Jenny had perched on the bed beside her aunt. Now she took one of the hands lying idle on the coverlet and held it between her own. 'Look,' she said persuasively, 'why not let this man take a look at you? If you don't like him you can say so and then you need not see him again——and as for the small fortune, you know quite well that you could pay a dozen professors and hardly notice it.' She lifted her aunt's hand up to her cheek for a moment. 'To please me?' she coaxed.

'Oh, very well,' agreed her aunt grumpily. 'You're just like your mother, she could charm water from a stone. But mind you, if I don't like him, I shall tell him so.' She stared at Jenny for a moment and added in a confused way: 'I don't feel very well, Jenny.'

'No, I know, my dear, but you will feel better,

I promise you, and I'll stay with you. Now will you rest for a little while? I'm going to talk to Doctor Toms for a few minutes and then I'll come back and sit with you.'

Miss Creed nodded, seeing nothing unusual in the fact that someone should forgo their night's sleep in order to keep her company; she wasn't a selfish woman, but she had been used to having her own way and people to carry out her wishes without question for so long that the idea that it might be inconvenient for them to do so never crossed her mind.

Jenny waited until her aunt had closed her eyes and then followed the doctor out of the room, closing the door softly for her aunt had sharp ears.

'She's ill, isn't she?' she whispered, and when the doctor nodded. 'Can you get this professor quickly?'

Doctor Toms nodded again. 'By sheer good fortune he happens to be spending some days with me—we've been friends for some years and he has been lecturing at Bristol; he still has several lectures to give, so he won't be going back for a week or so.'

'Back where?'

'Holland. He's Dutch.'

Jenny frowned, her mind vaguely filled with windmills, canals and bottles of gin. 'Oh—Is he all right? Clever, I mean.'

'Brilliant,' said Doctor Toms. 'You know what I suspect your aunt has?'

'Subdural haematoma,' hazarded Jenny.

He looked surprised and then said: 'Of course you come across them pretty often. I'm not sure, of course, that's why I would like Professor van Draak te Solendijk to see her.'

Jenny's eyes opened very wide. 'Good grief, what a frightful name!'

The doctor smiled faintly. 'Everyone calls him van Draak.'

'Thank goodness for that. Aunt may not like him.'

Her companion smiled again. 'I fancy she will. Now I must get back home. I'll be here round about nine o'clock in the morning, but telephone if you're worried. What about your sleep?'

'I'll doze and get Florrie up between six and seven—that'll give me a chance to have a bath and breakfast.' She smiled at him. 'Thanks for letting me know, Doctor Toms. Poor Aunt Bess, we must get her better.'

Her aunt was dozing restlessly when she went back into the room. Jenny settled herself in a chair, kicking off her shoes and arranging the table lamp so that it didn't disturb the bed's occupant. She was hungry and longed for a cup of tea, but she would have to wait for it. She had no intention of disturbing Florrie or anyone else at that hour. They must have had a busy, worrying time of it—besides, she had told Aunt Bess that she would stay with her. She settled herself as comfortably as possible and prepared to sit out the rest of the night.

CHAPTER TWO

MISS CREED seemed a little better in the morning, but Jenny, making her ready for the day, wasn't too happy about her, but there were things she had to do. She left Aunt Bess in Florrie's capable hands and went away to unpack her things, have a bath and change her clothes. Doctor Toms arrived just as she was finished breakfast and took her back upstairs with him while he examined his patient again, made a few non-committal remarks which only served to make her snort indignantly and then took Jenny aside to explain worriedly that there was an urgent maternity case he had to go to, but that the professor would be over at the earliest possible moment on his return from Yeovil hospital where he had been delivering a series of lectures to post-graduates. He went away then, warning Jenny that it seemed very likely that her aunt would have to go to hospital herself.

Jenny set about making her aunt as comfortable as possible while she kept an ever watchful eye on her condition. There was no dramatic change, but certainly it was deteriorating steadily. Soon after one o'clock Florrie came to relieve her for her lunch, and stayed while Jenny did a brisk round of the old house, making sure that everything was ready for the visitors. The clock tower chimed twice as she went through the door in the entrance hall and up the circular stairs which led to the lobby on the next floor, and the private wing.

There was someone in the lobby and the small apartment seemed crowded by reason of the vast size of the man standing there, and he wasn't only large, but tall too, with iron-grey hair and bright blue eyes, and although he wasn't young he was nonetheless handsome. Jenny spared a second to register that fact before saying pleasantly:

'I think you must have missed your way; this leads to the private part of the house.'

She was affronted by his cool: 'I am well aware of that, young lady—perhaps you would tell whoever is looking after Miss Creed that I am here. Professor van Draak.'

'Te Solendijk,' added Jenny, who had a splendid memory for names. 'I'm looking after her, I'm her niece, Janet Wren, so perhaps you'll tell me anything I should know when you've seen her—treatment and so on,' she pointed out kindly, for he looked so surprised.

His thick eyebrows lifted. 'I hardly think I need to discuss these things with you, Miss. . .er. . .it is surely not your business.'

He had a deep voice, probably a delight to

listen to when he was in a good mood, which he was not, Jenny decided. She turned her head to look out of the window at the small groups of people coming along the drive towards the entrance and spoke over her shoulder. 'Of course it's my business; Miss Creed is my aunt and I shall be nursing her. You have no reason to be so cross, you know.'

He stared down his arrogant nose at her. 'I am not cross, young lady. I do not allow my feelings to take control of me at any time.'

Her eyes widened. 'You poor soul,' she exclaimed warmly, 'it must be like walking about in a plastic bag!'

He didn't smile, although his eyes gleamed beneath their heavy lids. 'You are foolish, Miss Wren, for in that case I should be dead.'

'That's what I meant.' She delivered this telling shot with a sweet smile and opened the door. 'If you would come with me, Professor. . .'

He stalked down the corridor beside her, making no attempt to speak, and Jenny, keeping up as best she could, was quite relieved when they reached her aunt's room. At the door, before she opened it, he said evenly: 'You do understand that Doctor Toms was unable to come with me—it is a little unusual. . .'

'Not to worry,' Jenny told him cheerfully, 'he's an old family friend, you know. Aunt Bess won't mind,' she paused, 'unless you do?'

'It is usual for the patients' own doctor to be present,' he pointed out in his almost faultless English. 'I am a foreigner—your aunt. . .'

'Oh, don't worry about that.' She spoke reassuringly. 'She doesn't like foreigners as a rule, but I expect she'll like you.'

She was about to open the door when his hand came down on hers, preventing her. 'Why do you say that?'

She smiled at him, wishing he didn't look so unfriendly. 'You look the part,' she told him, and when he took his hand away, opened the door.

Florrie, with a few urgent whispers to Jenny, went away, and Miss Creed said sharply from the bed: 'Jenny? Where have you been? And when is that foreigner coming?'

'He's here now,' said the Professor, his manner so changed that Jenny looked at him in surprise. He didn't look angry and withdrawn any more, but calm and assured, a rock for any patient to lean upon and pour out their symptoms. His voice was gentle too and although nothing could alter the masterful angle of his nose, his manner was such to win the confidence of the most cantankerous of patients. He had walked across the room, to stand by the bed in full view of his patient while Jenny introduced him, returning Miss Creed's fierce stare with a mild look which Jenny found hard to believe.

'You will forgive me,' said the Professor

suavely, that I should come in this fashion without
our mutual friend Doctor Toms. I believe he has
explained the circumstances to Miss. . .er. . .' He
paused and looked enquiringly at Jenny, who
gave him a stony stare and didn't utter a sound;
if he wanted to call her Miss Er for the rest of
their acquaintance, then let him! She got her own
back presently, though.

'Doctor Toms has told Professor van Draak—
oh, dear what a very long name—te Solendijk all
about you, Aunt Bess. Do you want me to stay?'

Two pairs of blue eyes were turned upon her,
two mouths, firm to the point of stubbornness,
snapped: 'Of course.' They should get on
famously, the pair of them, thought Jenny, casting
her own eyes meekly downwards.

The Professor took his time; he was not to be
hurried by Miss Creed's voice, bossy still though
weak and slurred, telling him what to do and what
not to do. When at length he was finished, she
snapped: 'Well, what's the matter with me? Or
is it just a headache—though I daresay you'll
make the most of it, whatever it is.'

The Professor ignored that, straightening himself slowly and eyeing her with calm. 'Yes, it is
a headache, but that is only a symptom of its
cause. I should like to operate on you, Miss Creed.
Would you go into hospital?'

'No. To be mauled about and pay hundreds of
pounds for something an aspirin will cure.'

He said impassively: 'I'm afraid aspirin won't cure this headache.' He gave her a long, considered look and she stared back at him defiantly, although it obviously needed an effort; Aunt Bess was pushing herself to her limit. He went on deliberately: 'If I don't operate, Miss Creed, you will die.'

'Plain speaking.'

'I don't think you will listen to anything else. I shouldn't myself.'

'You will tell me exactly what I have wrong with me and what my chances of living are.'

'Certainly. You wish Miss. . .?'

'Er,' murmured Jenny helpfully. 'I'm a nurse and I shall be looking after my aunt, Professor van Draak.'

'Ah, yes—just so. Then I will explain.'

Which he did very nicely; a minute haemorrhage in the brain, at present only causing severe headaches; difficulty with speech, with breathing, blackouts. . .'You will have had those, of course?' he asked offhand, and nodded when Aunt Bess said quite meekly that yes, she had had several. 'I shall find the site of the haemorrhage,' said the Professor, not boastfully but as a man who was quite sure that he would, 'repair it, and provided you do exactly as you are told, you will be as good as new within a very short space of time.'

Miss Creed considered his words. 'It sounds

reasonable enough,' she said drowsily, 'but I'm too tired to decide today—come and see me tomorrow.'

He put his handsome head on one side, contemplating her. 'I should like to operate tonight,' he told her calmly.

The lined, elderly face on the pillow lost some of its firmness. 'Tonight?'

He nodded. 'The sooner the better. I can arrange through Doctor Toms to have the use of the theatre at Cowper's,' the local cottage hospital and not so very far away. 'You would have to remain there as a patient, but I promise you that the moment you are fit enough to move, you shall return here.'

'Jenny?' Miss Creed suddenly sounded very elderly indeed. 'What shall I do, Jenny?'

'Just what the Professor asks, Aunt Bess,' Jenny had been standing at the bedside, opposite the Professor, but she had taken no part in the conversation. Now she came a little nearer. 'Doctor Toms says that Professor van Draak is a brilliant man, and you know you will only have the best—besides,' she went on cunningly, 'you'll be as right as a trivet by the time Oliver comes to stay.' Which wasn't quite true, but she judged that a small fib was justified in the circumstances.

She watched her aunt thinking about it and nobody spoke until Miss Creed said: 'Get on with it, then.' Her voice was suddenly strong and auto-cratic. 'And be sure and make a good job of it.'

The Professor assured her levelly that he would do just that, adding: 'Might I have a few words with Miss...your niece? Perhaps someone could be fetched to sit with you for a short time.'

'Do what you like,' said Miss Creed rudely. 'I can see that you're a man who always wants his own way Jenny, don't let him flatten you.'

As they walked back along the corridor, Jenny said: 'Aunt Bess doesn't feel well...' and was cut short by his patient: 'My dear young lady, no one with a subdural haemorrhage feels well, and if you are referring to her remark that you should not allow me to flatten you, I rather imagine that there would be little possibility of that.'

She stopped so suddenly that he, walking a little behind her and to one side, bumped into her and was forced to catch her by the shoulders to steady her. She brushed him away with a wave of one beautifully kept hand. 'I can't imagine why you are so rude, Professor. Do you dislike the English, or just women? Whichever it is, isn't going to help Aunt Bess very much.'

'My dear Miss...'

'Look,' she interrupted him impatiently, 'the name's Wren—quite easy and so much nicer than Er.'

He laughed then, and for the first time she realised with a little shock that when he laughed

he looked quite different—years younger; someone she would like to know. . . She squashed
the thought at once and prompted: 'You were
saying?'

He had stopped laughing and was looking
down his nose again, holding the door open for
her at the head of the little staircase. 'Merely that
I do not dislike the English, nor, for that matter,
women. I hope your curiosity is satisfied?'

'Pooh!' exclaimed Jenny, and ran down the
stairs very fast, but despite his size, he was at the
bottom only inches behind her, to open the door
and usher her politely into the entrance hall.
'Where can we talk?' he asked abruptly.

She led the way through the small groups of
people wandering round, out of the door and
turned down a little flagged path which led to the
tiny church adjacent to the house. Through the
churchyard gate, among the ancient tombstones,
she said: 'Here.'

Rather to her surprise he remarked: 'A peaceful
and quite beautiful spot,' and then leaned himself
against the old grey walls of the church, crossed
his elegantly shod feet, dug his hands into his
jacket pockets and went on: 'Your aunt is very
ill; the thing is to get to the haemorrhage before
it does any further damage; any moment it could
worsen, although somehow I don't think it will,
but we mustn't take chances. If I can operate
quickly she has a very good chance of recovery.'

He glanced at the paper thin gold watch on his wrist. 'It is now three o'clock. I have already spoken to Cowper's; the theatre is available at six o'clock. Doctor Toms will be there, of course, and I have an excellent anaesthetist standing by as well as an extremely able assistant. Will you telephone for an ambulance and bring Miss Creed to the hospital at once? I presume that you will stay there until the operation is over.'

'Of course. I must see Mrs Thorpe—the vicar's wife, you know, and our housekeeper. . .' Jenny was half talking to herself and he looked amused. 'The ambulance first, of course, but don't I have to have your authority for that?'

'I talked to them a short time ago; they are more or less expecting a call for an urgent case, so there should be no difficulty.'

She eyed him curiously. 'You were so sure— you had everything arranged.'

'I like to be prepared—besides, I respect Doctor Toms' judgment, I merely confirmed what he strongly suspected.'

She said inanely: 'Yes, well. . .I suppose so. Have you a car here?'

He nodded in the direction of a magnificent Panther J72 drawn up on the gravel sweep outside the entrance and she opened her eyes wide. 'Is that yours? I thought. . .that is, I. . .'

'An unlikely car for a not-so-young Dutchman.' He smiled faintly.

'No—yes—I mean, she's a beauty.' She was suddenly a little breathless. 'And you're not even middle-aged!'

'Forty, as near as not—and you, Miss Wren?'

'Me? I'm twenty-five.' She hadn't meant to tell him that. 'Where shall I take Aunt Bess?'

'They will be expecting her. The usual routine before operation—nothing to eat or drink—but of course you know that.' They were walking towards his car as he spoke and after the briefest of goodbyes, Jenny went indoors to telephone and then see Florrie and Mrs Thorpe. There was no time to lose, but even in her haste she found herself wishing that she could have spared a moment to watch the Professor drive off his splendid car.

Florrie grasped the situation within minutes; Jenny knew that she would be able to leave everything in her capable hands. The same couldn't be said for Mrs Thorpe, who wasted precious minutes exclaiming: 'There, I only said to Mr Thorpe yesterday,' and 'Well, I never,' and 'It's to be hoped—' She would have gone on for some time in this tiresome manner if Jenny hadn't cut her politely short, begged her to organise the visitors on the following afternoon and arrange for Baxter to sell tickets again.

'Probably I shall be back by then, Mrs Thorpe, but I'll let you know. Mrs Trott'—Trott was the elderly lodgekeeper-cum-handyman—'said she

would help out if it was necessary at any time,
and I'm sure she will—it will only be for a day
or two while I'm with my aunt.'

Mrs Thorpe looked important. 'Now, don't
worry about anything, Jenny, I'll see to everything.' Her bosom swelled alarmingly. 'None of
us would dream of letting Miss Creed down.'

Jenny thanked her nicely, glad that her aunt
couldn't hear her doing it, for she had no opinion
at all of the vicar's wife, although she used that
lady's services quite unscrupulously whenever it
suited her to do so, and hurried back to her aunt's
room. Miss Creed hadn't been told that she would
be leaving almost immediately; the ambulance
Jenny had telephoned for would be arriving very
shortly. She sent the devoted Florrie away, found
an overnight bag, rammed in what she considered
necessary for her aunt's comfort and approached
the bed.

Aunt Bess had her eyes shut, but she spoke
immediately in a slurred voice. 'Don't imagine
that I don't know that you're arranging something
behind my back, Jenny, because I'm perfectly
aware of it.'

'Yes, Aunt Bess, I'm sure you are, but it's
nothing you haven't been consulted about. The
Professor wants you in hospital—he told you that
just now—and I'm packing your bag to take with
you. The ambulance will be here in a few
minutes.'

'I'm perfectly able. . .' began Miss Creed.

'No, dear, you're not—not just at present. I'm coming with you and I shall stay for a bit. Everything's arranged, so there's no need for you to worry about a thing.'

'I'm not worried,' stated her aunt drowsily. 'You're sure that that enormous man knows what he's doing?'

'Yes, Aunt, I am.' Jenny, to her own surprise, discovered that she really was sure about that, which seemed a little silly considering that she had never seen him operate.

And hours later, when he came straight from theatre, still in his green smock and trousers, his grey hair hidden by his cap, to find her in Sister's office, waiting, she was just as sure.

He said without preamble: 'Your aunt will be all right. She's very fit for her age and should make a good recovery, although she will have to take reasonable care. Do you want the details?'

'Please.'

He gave them at some length and then said: 'Miss Creed should regain consciousness shortly. She will want to see you, will she not? You are prepared to stay?'

'Of course. They've very kindly arranged for the night.'

'Good. I'll be around for a while and I shall be in early in the morning. Doctor Toms had to go straight from theatre. He's quite satisfied.'

She looked at him rather shyly. 'Thank you, Professor van Draak, I'm very grateful,' and felt snubbed when he replied coldly: 'You have no need to be; it is my work.' He opened the door, preparatory to leaving. 'Someone will fetch you very shortly.'

He had gone, leaving her feeling that even if he didn't like her, and it seemed that he didn't, he might have been a little less terse. But he hadn't been terse with Aunt Bess, he had been kind and patient and moreover clever enough to see exactly how contrary she was, and deal with it in the only way she would accept. Jenny had seen her aunt make mincemeat of those who crossed her will too many times not to know that she was the last person to listen to cajoling or persuasion. She got to her feet and walked up and down the little room. Well, the man was a professor of surgery; presumably professors had that little extra something that set them above the rest. She stopped in front of a mirror and poked at her hair in an absent-minded fashion. All the same, he was arrogant and much too indifferent in his manner. She wondered if he were married and if so, if he were happy, although it was no business of hers. Only it had been providential that he happened to be staying with Doctor Toms, for Cowpers, excellent though it was was too small to have consultants attached to its staff and it would have meant her aunt travelling miles to

Bristol or Poole or Southampton. As it was he had
been allowed to make use of the small hospital's
theatre. She had noticed that he was known to
the staff there, too. Possibly he had stayed with
Doctor Toms before and come to know the staff
there—she would have to ask Doctor Toms.

A nurse came to fetch her then and she went
along to the back of the hospital, where the three
private rooms were. Miss Creed was in the first
of these, surrounded by a variety of equipment,
looking very shrunken and frail. She opened her
eyes as Jenny went in, smiled a little and closed
them again, but presently she said in a thread of
a voice: 'All over?'

Jenny sat down by the bed. She had been keeping a tight check on her feelings, for Aunt Bess
loathed emotion or tears. Now she could have
wept with sheer relief, but she managed a steady:
'Yes, my dear, and very satisfactory, too,' aware
as she said it that the Professor had come in
silently and was standing behind her. He said
something low-voiced to the nurse and went to
the foot of the bed. Miss Creed opened her eyes
again. 'Pleased with your handiwork?' she asked
in a woolly voice.

'Yes, I am, Miss Creed, and you will be too
in a very short time. Nurse is going to give you
an injection and I should like you to go to
sleep again.'

His patient submitted an arm. 'No choice,'

she muttered, and then: 'Don't go, Jenny.'

'No, Aunt Bess, I'll be here when you wake.'

So she sat in the chair through the night's long hours, fortified by cups of strong tea the nurses brought her from time to time, trying to keep awake in ease Aunt Bess should wake and want her. But her aunt slept on and towards morning Jenny let her heavy lids drop over her tired eyes and dozed herself, to be wakened gently by the Professor's hand on her shoulder, and his voice, very quiet in her ear. 'Your aunt's regaining consciousness.' And when she sat up, her copper head tousled and no make-up left on her face at all, he whispered, 'You're tired. You will go to bed when your aunt has spoken to you; I would send you away now, but of course she won't remember those few brief moments directly after the operation. You can return later on.' And when she would have protested: 'They will let you have a bed here for a few hours.'

It had been worth the long tedious wait. Aunt Bess opened her eyes and spoke in a normal voice. 'Good girl,' and then: 'Where's that man?'

'Here,' answered the Professor quietly. 'Everything is quite satisfactory, Miss Creed. I want you to sleep as much as you can. Jenny must go to bed now, she has been up all night.'

'We're fond of each other,' said Aunt Bess in a quite strong voice. 'I'd do the same for her. But send her to bed, by all means.' Her voice faded a little and then revived. 'You will anyway, whatever I say.'

'Yes. She shall come back when she has rested; you will feel more like talking then.'

Jenny found herself whisked away to an empty room in the pleasant nurses' home adjoining the hospital. She wasn't sure of the time, and she was too tired to care. She had a bath, drank the tea one of the nurses brought her, and fell into bed, asleep the moment her head touched the pillow.

She was wakened by one of the day Sisters. 'Your aunt is asking for you,' she was told. 'I'm sorry to wake you like this, but she's being a little difficult—you could come?'

Jenny shook the sleep from her head. 'Yes, of course. Is she worse?'

'No—just unable to settle and not very operative. Here's a dressing gown and slippers—you don't mind? We can go through the passage.'

Jenny wrapped herself in the voluminous garment, several sizes too big for her, and thrust her feet into equally large slippers and allowed herself to be led through the covered way to the hospital. 'What's the time?' she asked, half way there.

'Not quite midday. If you could persuade your aunt to have an injection. . . We'll bring you a light meal and you could go to sleep again. You must be worn out.'

'I'm fine,' declared Jenny sturdily, and stifled

a yawn as she lifted dark, delicately arched brows at the sound of her aunt's voice, raised in wrath.

And indeed she was in an ill humour; flushed as well, sitting up against her pillows, her blue eyes brilliant under her bandaged head. 'There you are!' she cried imperiously. 'And where have you been, may I ask—leaving me to these silly girls? And where's that foreigner? I thought he was here to look after me? Heaven knows I shall be expected to pay him a king's ransom.'

Jenny perched beside the bed. 'I was having a nap, Aunt Bess—I sat with you during the night and I was a bit sleepy. And Professor van Draak was here for most of the night too, he must have been tired after operating. What's worrying you, Aunt?'

Miss Creed moved her head restlessly. 'I want to go home,' she stated. 'I'm sick and tired of these people, all shouting at me to have an injection; I do not want to sleep.'

Jenny sighed soundlessly. 'Look, dear, you've had an operation and of course you don't feel quite the thing, and until you have a nice long sleep you won't feel much better. We know you don't feel sleepy, but the injection will send you off in no time. . .'

'And what's he doing here?' interrupted Miss Creed, looking past Jenny's shoulder.

The Professor had loomed up beside Jenny. He said now in his calm way: 'I've come to give

you your injection, Miss Creed—your niece has
explained why you should have it.' He nodded
to Jenny to hold her Aunt's arm firmly and slid
the needle in without further ado.

'I'm not accustomed to being treated in this
manner,' his patient began angrily. 'I like my own
way. . .'

'And so do I,' agreed the Professor pleasantly.
'You will feel much more yourself when you
wake up—tired and not inclined to do much, but
much more comfortable in your head.'

'Bah. . .' began Aunt Bess, the lids falling over
her tired eyes, 'I don't believe. . .'

Jenny heaved a sigh of relief. 'Poor dear, she
must be feeling ghastly,' she said softly, and went
on sitting where she was, overcome by tiredness
once more. She yawned hugely, pushed up the
sleeves of the ridiculous dressing gown and lifted
her arms to sweep back her tide of hair, hanging
all over the place. She would have gone to sleep
then and there if the Professor hadn't said in a
cold voice, 'Go back to your bed, Miss Wren. I
see that you are still in need of sleep.' His tone
was so very icy that she opened her eyes to take
a look at him. His face looked icy too, the brows
drawn together in a frown.

'Fallen down on the job, have I?' she asked
pertly, tiredness forgotten for the moment in a
wish to annoy him. He had been up most of the
night too, but he didn't look as though he had;

he was probably one of those iron-willed men who didn't allow himself to feel tired or happy or sad or anything else. . . She opened her mouth to tell him so, but yawned instead and fell asleep, sitting upright, swaying a little.

The Professor looked more annoyed than ever. 'Will you open the door, Nurse?' he asked the student left to sit with Miss Creed, and swept Jenny up into his arms as though she were a tiresome child and carried her back down the covered passage, to put her gently on her bed and pull the blanket over her. Jenny, dead to the world, rolled over. If she had been awake to hear his: 'Troublesome girl, to plague me so,' uttered in a cold voice, she would most certainly have answered him with spirit. As it was she gave a delicate snore.

CHAPTER THREE

JENNY didn't wake until almost four o'clock and then lay for a few minutes gathering her still sleepy wits. She supposed she should get up; she had had another three hours' sleep and possibly, if her aunt was better, she would be able to go back to Dimworth later on in the evening.

But when she found her way to Aunt Bess's room presently, she found Sister there once more, and as she stood in the doorway, wondering if she should go in or not, she was lifted neatly out of the way by the Professor, who took no notice of her at all, but went straight to the bedside, where he bent over Miss Creed, murmuring to Sister with an infuriating softness, so that Jenny, very worried by now, couldn't hear a word. She was on the point of asking what was the matter when he spoke without turning his head. 'Come in, Miss Wren. I have something to say to you.'

She went to stand by him, looking first at his face and then at her aunt's, calm and unconscious. The look on her face caused him to say quickly: 'No need to get alarmed; your aunt has had a relapse. We're going to give her some more blood and change the electrolytes—I think that should put things right. She hasn't been as quiet as she should.'

'No danger?' asked Jenny anxiously.

'I think not.' He gave her a considered look and she said at once:

'May I stay here with her? I've had a good sleep, perhaps if I'm here when she comes round, I could persuade her to take things easy for a few days. She's rather strong-willed.'

He smiled faintly. 'Sister has had quite a difficult time of it this afternoon, I'm sure she will be glad of your help.' He glanced across the bed to where Sister stood. 'Perhaps Miss Wren could have a meal now and relieve you and nurse? I see no reason why she shouldn't sit up with her aunt, she has had a good rest.'

Jenny's charming bosom swelled with indignation. A good rest, indeed! Two periods of sleep of barely three hours on top of a night sitting up in a chair after driving down from London—the man wasn't only made of iron himself, he expected everyone else to be the same. She was willing to stay up for an endless succession of nights for Aunt Bess, she conceded illogically, but he assumed too much. She was in two minds to refuse a meal, just to show her independence, but she would probably be famished if she did. She said, outwardly meek, 'I'll be glad to do that, Sister, if you agree to it.'

So she was given her meal and installed in a

chair by Aunt Bess's bed, primed with instructions and with the promise of relief for half an hour round about midnight. There wasn't much chance to sit down, though, what with half-hourly observations and keeping an eye on the drips. Adjusting them, Jenny thought that when her aunt wakened, she would want to know about those and probably do her best to remove them. Marking up her charts neatly, she sincerely hoped not.

The evening passed quietly. Aunt Bess showed no sign of rousing. The Professor arrived again about nine o'clock, this time with Doctor Toms, examined his patient, nodded distantly to Jenny and went again.

'And good riddance,' declared Jenny as the door shut quietly behind him, and then jumped visibly as it opened again. 'I heard that,' declared the Professor in his turn.

The hospital was quiet; the nights usually were, for casualties went to Yeovil and the patients, for the most part, slept for the greater part of the night. The night staff, small but efficient, managed very well, calling up the day nurses if anything dire occurred. About midnight Night Sister put her head round the door. 'Everything OK?' She smiled in acknowledgement of Jenny's nod and whispered: 'Someone will relieve you in a few minutes,' and went her soft-footed way, to be followed almost at once by a student nurse. Jenny ate a hurried meal and went back once more and the nurse, whispering that the patient hadn't stirred, crept away.

It was two o'clock in the morning, just as Jenny was changing a drip, that her aunt opened her eyes and said in a normal voice 'You should be in bed,' and then: 'I feel a great deal better.'

'Good,' said Jenny, 'and so you will if you stay very quiet, Aunt Bess. And I've been to bed, so don't bother about me.' She smiled down at her aunt, trying to be matter-of-fact and casual, because Aunt Bess hated tears or a display of emotion. 'How about a drink?'

She was giving it when the Professor came silently into the room, smiled at his patient and put out a hand for the charts.

He studied them carefully, grunted his approval and gave them back to Jenny without looking at her. 'You're better,' he told Aunt Bess, 'well enough for me to explain why you must lie quiet for a little longer.' And he explained very simply, in a quiet voice before adding: 'I should like you to go to sleep again now, but if you find that impossible will you lie still and relax, then there will be no need to give you another injection at present. Your niece will prop you up a little more, I think. . .'

'Don't you go to bed either?' asked Aunt Bess.

'Oh, certainly.' He smiled again and strolled to the door. 'I'll be in to see you again after breakfast.' His hand was on the door handle when he said: 'Miss Wren, will you hand me the charts? There are one or two things I should like to alter. Sister will return them presently.' He barely glanced at her and she supposed that she deserved it.

Aunt Bess went to sleep after that, remarking with some of her old tartness that Jenny and the Professor didn't seem to be on the best of terms, and Jenny, sitting in her chair once more, trying to keep awake for the last hours of the night, couldn't help but agree with her.

She was in bed and asleep very soon after the day staff came on duty, so that she missed Professor van Draak's visits in the morning, and in the afternoon he brought Sister with him, just as though Jenny were a visitor, and waited pointedly until she had gone out of the room before he examined her aunt. However, he joined her presently in the corridor, reassured her as to her aunt's condition, gave it as his opinion that she was now out of danger, and suggested that there was no need for Jenny to stay the night. 'I shall be passing Dimworth as I return to Doctor Toms,' he remarked without much warmth. 'I could give you a lift.'

It would have been nice to have refused him, but she hadn't much choice; there would be no one free at Dimworth to fetch her and she had no intention of telephoning Toby. She thanked him with a chilliness to equal his own and went back to sit with Aunt Bess.

Her aunt didn't seem to mind her going—indeed, she began to give a great number of messages, repeated several times in a muddled fashion, and added a list as long as her arm of tasks to be done at Dimworth, falling asleep in the middle of it. Jenny kissed the tired, still determined face and went out to where the Professor would be waiting for her. He got out and opened the car door for her and she had barely settled in her seat before he was driving away.

Jenny, having difficulty with her safety belt, said crossly: 'You don't like me at all, do you, Professor?' and was furious at his laugh.

It was a nasty laugh, full of mockery and the wrong kind of amusement, and his: 'My dear girl, you flatter yourself, and me too—I have no interest in you at all, although to be quite honest I must admit that I haven't much time for tart young women with red hair.'

'I expect you pride yourself on being plain-spoken,' said Jenny sweetly. 'I call it rude. Just by way of interest, what kind of girl do you like?'

He allowed the car to slow and shot a sidelong glance at her. 'Tall, calm, sweet-tempered—with good looks, of course; fair hair, blue eyes, a pleasant voice. . .'

'A cardboard creature,' cried Jenny, 'and even if you did find her, she'd be a dead bore as a

wife.' A thought struck her. 'Have you found her?
Perhaps you're married.'

'What an impertinent girl you are.' He spoke
quite pleasantly. 'No, I am not married. When do
you intend to visit your aunt again?'

A neat snub, if ever there was one. 'I'll drive
over after breakfast. When do you return to
Holland?'

'Wishful thinking?' he enquired. 'When your
aunt is recovered.'

Jenny shifted in her seat, uncomfortably aware
that she hadn't expressed nearly enough gratitude.
'Oh no. . .well, I'd like to thank you for what
you've done for Aunt Bess. I know you saved
her life and I'm deeply grateful—I hope it hasn't
spoilt your holiday here.'

It was a nice little speech which he completely
ruined. 'I get paid for it, you know,' he reminded
her smoothly, 'and I haven't been on holiday.'

Jenny exploded with temper. 'You're impossible! We're right back where we started, aren't
we? I've never met. . . You have no need to. . .'
She drew a deep breath and swallowed the
temper. 'What a lovely day it is,' she observed
brightly.

The Professor's eyes gleamed momentarily and
a muscle twitched at the corner of his firm mouth
as he agreed suavely before launching into a
businesslike discussion upon Miss Creed's illness. And at the house he refused her polite

invitation to come in for a drink, and without pretending an excuse either.

She dismissed him from her thoughts the moment she was in the house, and indeed forgot about him entirely while she listened to Florrie's account of what had been happening during her absence—nothing much, it seemed. A good attendance on both days; they had run out of homemade jam; Mrs Thorpe had been far too bossy and annoyed Grimshaw...

Jenny lent a sympathetic ear, made a few tactful suggestions, praised Florrie, gave an expurgated account of her aunt's illness and went round the house. The rooms which were open to the public were exactly as they should be; she checked the burglar alarm and then went along to her aunt's room to collect a few more things she might require while she was in hospital, then went out of the side door, to take a short cut through the gardens and park to the vicarage. Mrs Thorpe might have been bossy, but she was kindhearted and well-meaning. Jenny found her at home, said all that was necessary, thanked her with charm and set off to the house once more. Supper and bed would be nice.

Aunt Bess was better in the morning. Jenny, herself rested after a good night's sleep, viewed her relative's still pale face with satisfaction. The relapse had been overcome: it was now just a question of the patient doing exactly as she was told to do. And for the next few days that was just what she did, much to Jenny's surprise, mildly accepting what she described to her niece as slops—served up daintily on a tray, but still slops—and allowing the nurses to get her out of and into her bed with the minimum of fuss. Jenny was completely mystified as to her aunt's change of manner until several days after the operation when she happened to be in the room when the Professor paid his visit.

'It's the sixth day tomorrow,' her aunt pointed out when he had finished examining her. 'I've won.'

He leaned against the foot of the bed, laughing down at her. 'Not until tomorrow morning—noon, I think we decided? And how about a further three days? You suggest the amount.'

Miss Creed chuckled. 'You come here tomorrow and pay up and I'll let you know then.'

Jenny waited until he had gone, smiling charmingly at his patient and giving her nothing but a brief nod. 'What was all that about?'

Aunt Bess grinned at her. 'We had a little bet.'

Jenny's eyes opened wide. 'A bet? Aunt Bess. . .'

'Fifty pounds that I couldn't hold out until tomorrow on the revolting food I'm forced to eat and twenty on the side that I wouldn't do exactly as I was told about getting up and all the other tiresome things I'm forced to do.'

Jenny let out a breath. 'You mean to say he betted...he couldn't, it's not professional... he's...'

'Huh,' Aunt Bess was positively smirking, 'what's to stop him?' She said gleefully: 'I shall make it a hundred tomorrow and buy you a pretty dress with the winnings.'

It would be exactly the same as if he marched her into a shop and chose a dress off the peg and gave it to her. 'No—it's sweet of you, Aunt Bess, but I've heaps of clothes. Why don't you put it towards that dear little chest we saw in that shop in Sherbourne a few weeks ago? You said you wanted it for Oliver. . .'

'So I did. Clever girl—that's what I'll do. Telephone the shop tomorrow, Jenny, and tell them to send it to Dimworth. When is Oliver coming? I've forgotten.'

'Next week. Margaret telephoned this morning early. She wanted to know if they should come because you hadn't been well—Oliver's a bit noisy, she thinks.'

'What a silly young woman she is; he'll be a tonic about the place. Besides, I shall be away for part of his stay. Professor van Draak says that I should have a change—a week or two away— we'll discuss that later. Now run along, child, and see about that chest.'

So Jenny ran along, saw to the chest, kept an eye on the day's visitors, did her share of the

polishing and tidying up when they had gone, and
went back to the hospital in the evening. Her aunt
was asleep and doing very well, Sister told her.
She would be fit to go home soon, provided she
did as she was told to do. Professor van Draak
would decide exactly when. Jenny nodded,
dropped a kiss on the sleeping Miss Creed's cheek
and went out to where the Morgan was parked.

It was overshadowed by the Panther de Ville,
with the Professor at its wheel, looking disagree-
able. 'I don't seem to have seen you for some
time,' he commented as he got out to stand
beside her.

'Nice for you,' observed Jenny flippantly.
'Aunt Bess is much better, isn't she?'

'Yes.'

She waited for him to say something else, but
evidently he wasn't wasting his breath. 'You've
been betting with her,' she said severely. 'I've
never heard such nonsense.'

His smile made her wish that they liked each
other. 'But it worked, did it not, Jenny Wren?
Your aunt is a splendid woman but a shockingly
bad patient—it was necessary to use guile.'

Jenny laughed—she hadn't done that for days.
It bubbled up in a delicious trill, and the Professor
stared at her as though he had only just seen her,
his eyes hooded.

'When may she come home?' she asked.

'Another week, provided everything goes

well. You will continue to look after her?'

'Yes.'

He nodded. 'I understand that her small nephew will be coming to stay at Dimworth. You do realise that there must be no untoward noise—no shouting—nothing to disturb her.'

'Oliver is six, but he's a very sensible little boy,' Jenny defended her nephew. 'If I explain why he has to be quiet, then he'll be quiet.'

'He has no mother?'

She thought of Margaret, who from one point of view wasn't a mother at all. 'Oh, yes, he has—she'll be coming with him.'

He stood back a little. 'Don't let me keep you. I'm sure you want to get back. Goodnight.' His voice was coolly polite.

She got into the Morgan without a word and drove away very neatly, not looking at him at all. Two can be rude, she reminded herself.

The Panther overtook her five minutes later, creeping up behind and then tearing past, giving her no more than a glimpse of an arrogant nose in a profile which ignored her. She said 'Phoo!' loudly to relieve her feelings and resisted a useless urge to overtake him in her turn.

And her temper wasn't improved at all when she found Toby waiting for her at Dimworth. He was full of helpful offers to do this and that, warnings as to her health if she didn't get enough sleep or eat enough and rounded off his remarks by reminding her that she hadn't answered any of his letters and had she thought any more about marrying him.

'No, I have not,' snapped Jenny. 'With Aunt Bess so ill and so much to do, I've had not time to think at all, and anyway, I don't want to marry you, Toby.' She added a polite 'Thank you.'

He was like a rubber ball, bouncing back whatever was said or done to him. 'Oh, well—I daresay you're tired. Is there anything I can do?'

The thought crossed her mind that the Professor wouldn't have asked; he would have known what wanted doing and done it without bothering to ask her, and then gone home and left her in peace. She said wearily: 'No, Toby—look, I've had a busy day and I'm tired.'

'You'd like me to go?' He got up out of the chair where he had been lounging. 'Suits me, old girl, I've got to be up early to go over and see that horse Mother wants me to buy.' He laughed. 'And I like my eight hours sleep, you know.'

She managed a friendly goodnight, although he had made her irritable. Such a nice young man, everyone said, and just the right husband for her, Margaret had observed on her last visit to Dimworth. Well, he might be nice, and young too, but he was too easy-going by far. Jenny went along to the kitchen, carved herself a hunk of bread and a slab of cheese and then, feeling better for her meal, went to bed.

She didn't see the Professor for two or three days. Somehow he had just been or was expected at any moment when she visited her aunt, and on two occasions he actually passed her driving back from the hospital, ignoring her on both occasions. They met eventually, face to face in the hospital's entrance and when he stood aside for her to pass she stopped in front of him. 'So there you are,' she exclaimed forthrightly. 'I was beginning to wonder if you'd gone back to Holland and forgotten to mention it to anyone.'

He allowed himself the faint glimmer of a smile. 'I overtook you just outside the village yesterday.'

She allowed her eyes to open widely and said innocently: 'Did you really? I had no idea. . .I should be obliged if you would let me know how my aunt is getting on. Sister passes on any news, of course, but that's not very satisfactory.'

The smile had gone, he looked down his nose at her and said austerely: 'It is unfortunate that we have missed each other just lately. I left sufficient information with Sister, or so I imagined. However, since we have met, I can tell you that Miss Creed should be well enough to return home in a day or two now. She will need a period of convalescence which presumably you will arrange and then a brief change of air—something different—a cruise would be ideal, for she would not need to exert herself in any way unless she felt like it. Someone would have to accompany her, of course. You?'

Jenny hesitated. It would mean giving up her job and her independence too, at any rate for the time being. 'Yes, of course I'll go with her if she wants me to. I'll have to go up to Queen's and see about leaving. I'm afraid they won't keep my job open.'

He wasn't very interested. 'You must do whatever you think fit,' he observed casually. 'Perhaps it would be a good idea if you arranged that while she is still in hospital.'

She agreed rather unhappily. 'Yes, I'm going to see her now. Thank you for sparing the time to see me.'

She slid past him and went along to her aunt's room, where she put on a bright face for the benefit of the invalid; entered with enthusiasm into plans for Oliver's visit, assured her aunt that it was of no consequence at all if she gave up her post at Queen's, and that nothing would be nicer than a cruise.

Only that night, in the quiet of her own room, she allowed herself the luxury of a good weep. She had expected her aunt to take it for granted that she would leave hospital and look after her—indeed, she had promised that she would, but she had expected that Toby would have understood a little how she felt about it. His: 'Oh, that's splendid news, old girl. We'll settle things when you get back from your trip, shall we? Once you're away from that place you'll realise how silly you've been hanging on so long. It isn't as if you need the money, and dash it all, everyone expects us to marry and I'm ready and willing, what more could a girl want?' had done nothing to dispel her gloom. What more did she want? she asked herself, sitting up in bed, hugging her knees. Just to be allowed to make her own life, prove that she could earn her own living, find herself a husband. . .someone, she told herself fiercely, who wouldn't call her old girl.

Getting Aunt Bess home wasn't as bad as Jenny had anticipated; indeed her aunt demonstrated a meekness quite unlike her usual forceful self. She was installed in a room on the ground floor so that she could, as she put it, keep an eye on things, and there had been a tremendous upheaval moving her bed and furniture from the room on the first floor. But once this was done, everyone had to admit that it was most convenient, for the new bedroom had a small sitting room leading from it and here Aunt Bess would be able to spend her days, ruling Dimworth from her chair.

She had been home three days when Oliver and his mother arrived, driving in the old-fashioned Daimler with Jamie, her father's gardener, at the wheel, for Margaret had never learnt to drive herself. She looked quite beautiful, Jenny thought, watching her get out of the car, her golden hair smooth, her expensive outfit in the exact blue of her eyes. She didn't wait for Oliver but started to walk towards Jenny, leaving him to scramble out on his own.

'How I hate the journey down!' she began, and kissed her perfunctorily on her cheek. 'But Father will insist that I have the car. Oliver gets so restless—I have quite a headache.'

Jenny murmured sympathy although she didn't feel particularly that way and turned to receive a boisterous greeting from her small relative, just as pleased to see him as he was to see her again. 'Come on in,' she invited. 'Margaret, you have your usual rooms; I've put Oliver next to me and Jamie's at the lodge. Aunt Bess is resting.' She looked inquiringly at Margaret. 'You did explain to Oliver?'

'About Aunt Bess? Oh, vaguely—he's only a little boy. . .'

Jenny sighed inwardly. 'Oliver, listen to me. You have to be as quiet as a mouse, because Aunt Bess hasn't been well. Presently, when you've had some lemonade, we'll go into the churchyard and I'll tell you exactly why.'

Margaret wrinkled her patrician nose. 'Oh, Jenny, must you? The churchyard, I mean.'

'It's a very pleasant place, and I must get him to understand about Aunt Bess, then he'll be good about it. Won't you, Oliver?'

They had reached the private wing by now and

Jenny ushered the visitors into the sitting room where Felicity had already set the coffee tray. They were drinking it, while Oliver enjoyed his lemonade and a great many biscuits besides, when he said suddenly, 'I haven't seen Dobbs.' Dobbs was Miss Creed's chauffeur and Oliver's firm friend, and Jenny, glad of a respite from the trivial conversation she and Margaret were holding, said:

'He's in Canada, visiting his son. He'll be back in a day or two—we've all missed him dreadfully.'

'Don't ask so many questions, Oliver,' his mother begged. 'Jenny, I think I'll go to my room—is there someone to unpack for me?'

'Ethel. . .'

'Still here? She should have been pensioned off years ago.'

'Aunt Bess wouldn't do that, Margaret. She's been here longer than I can remember and she hasn't anywhere else to go. She does the mending and looks after Aunt Bess's clothes beautifully.'

Margaret brightened. 'Oh, does she? Good, she can look after my things.' She studied Jenny for a minute. 'Are you still working at that dreadful hospital?'

'I went up to London and resigned my job while Aunt Bess was still in hospital.' Jenny spoke quietly, still feeling unhappy about it.

'She'll need some help for a little while yet. I can always get another job.'

'I can't think why you don't marry Toby— he's so suitable. . .' Margaret looked her over. 'You're quite a pretty girl, you know, Jenny, and you dress very well. Don't you want to settle down?'

Jenny said no rather abruptly and asked about Margaret's health, a red herring which never failed to succeed, but Margaret had barely begun on her various little illnesses when Florrie opened the door and said in her nice cosy Somerset voice: 'The Professor's here, Miss Jenny—shall I ask him to come in here?'

Jenny frowned. He had said that he wouldn't be coming until the evening, but as usual he was doing as he pleased. 'Yes, do, Florrie—and perhaps you could send in some more coffee.'

She got to her feet as he came in and wished him a good morning and introduced Margaret. Margaret, she noted, had assumed her most beguiling air, reminding her of a Botticelli angel, and guaranteed to catch the eye of any man around. The Professor's eye was certainly caught; she gave him a few moments in which to feast his gaze before presenting Oliver.

She was a little surprised that the Professor behaved so nicely towards the little boy—indeed, his manner was that of a man entirely used to small boys, and when Oliver started to tell him about the pet rabbits he had left behind in Scotland, he listened with every sign of interest. It was Margaret who begged her son very prettily not to bore the visitor with his nonsense and then turned the conversation upon herself, while Jenny poured coffee and made what she always privately referred to as hostess murmurs. But presently when Margaret paused for breath, she asked him in businesslike tones if he had come to see her aunt, and if so, did he wish to do so at once, a remark which brought a decided twinkle to his eye.

'If it is convenient, yes. I have to go to Bristol this evening.' He looked at Margaret. 'It has been delightful meeting you,' he observed suavely, 'and I hope we may meet again before very long.'

And Jenny, watching, was aware of deep annoyance at this pretty speech; never once had he expressed a wish to see her again——on the contrary she had always had the distinct impression that he wished the reverse. It was wonderful what golden hair and blue eyes did to a man. She tossed her fiery mane over her shoulder and started for the door as he wished Oliver goodbye——in the nicest possible way, she was forced to admit.

Aunt Bess was awake and looking almost her usual self. 'You again!' she declared ungraciously. 'Heaven knows what your bill will be. I shall be forced to mortgage Dimworth. . .'

A remark which brought a crack of laughter from the Professor and a chuckle from Jenny. 'You share a sense of humour, at any rate,' observed Aunt Bess. 'Has Oliver arrived?'

'Yes, Aunt, he's downstairs having some lemonade.'

'Good—I'll see him when this fussing around is done with.' She threw a look at the Professor, taking her pulse. 'What do you think of the boy? You've seen him, of course?'

'Yes. A splendid little chap—a worthy heir to Dimworth.'

His patient nodded, well pleased. 'I think so too. And his mother?'

'A very beautiful woman.' His usually cool voice held warmth.

'I'll grant you that—not a patch on Jenny here, though.'

Jenny watched his brows lift faintly and a mocking little smile curve the corners of his mouth, and went a bright pink. By dint of holding her tongue firmly between her teeth she managed to say nothing at all. His bland, 'Er—I hardly feel in a position to say anything to that,' merely added to her discomfort.

To cover it she said a trifle tartly: 'Do you want to examine Aunt Bess, or is this just a social call?'

'Both, I hope, but if you're busy. . .?' His voice was very bland.

She said with dignity that she wasn't and

became strictly professional, addressing him—rather naughtily because she could see that it irritated him—as sir whenever she had the opportunity.

He came every day, although there was really no need now that his patient was doing so well, and it was more than coincidence that Margaret always seemed to be going in or coming out of the house when he arrived—and what more natural than that she should suggest a stroll in the gardens, or offer to show him the lily pond? Jenny, up to her eyes in visitors; getting ready for them and clearing up after them, still had time to notice that, and Aunt Bess, sitting in her great chair by the window and missing nothing, remarked with some asperity: 'Setting her cap at him, isn't she? Should have thought he would have had more sense.'

'It would be nice for Oliver,' said Jenny thoughtfully as she laboriously unpicked the knitting Miss Creed had mangled.

Her aunt gave her a long look she didn't see. 'Indeed it would; he needs a father. Eduard seems to like children.'

So it was Eduard now. Jenny speared a stitch with violence. 'A pity he hasn't married, then,' she observed lightly.

'Time enough, my dear, time enough. If you've finished with that knitting I wish you would go along and see how Grimshaw is managing with those pictures. I know he's good at those sort of jobs, but he's getting on a bit. And I'd like Oliver to come and sit with me for a bit.'

Jenny bent to kiss her aunt's cheek. 'OK—but I'll have to find him first; I bet he's up a tree.'

He was. She coaxed him down, warned him to be good and quiet and sent him on his way before going to find Grimshaw, who was managing very nicely. It was on her way back from this mission that she saw Margaret and the Professor. Margaret had a hand tucked confidently in his arm and was laughing up into his face as they strolled along the broad walk along the south face of the house. She had told Jenny the previous evening that she was enjoying her visit far more than she had ever done before. Watching her now, Jenny could see why.

CHAPTER FOUR

THE Professor, calling each day, yet managed to avoid meeting Jenny alone, and when they did see each other it was in Aunt Bess's company, listening to her giving dictatorial directions concerning her own welfare, the running of the house, and her forthcoming holiday. She had decided finally upon a cruise, the Professor having cunningly made sure that she did so by stating that possibly she would find it much too tiring. Madeira, she had settled for, and the Canaries—she hadn't been there for many years and she had a mind to see them again.

Jenny was to go with her, of course; Aunt Bess hadn't bothered to enquire about her niece's job at Queen's, she had taken it for granted that any sacrifice which Jenny made would be done willingly and for her benefit. And she had suddenly become quite overbearing about Toby. Whenever she and Jenny were alone, he was always the topic of conversation, it was as though Miss Creed took it for granted that Jenny wanted to marry him, despite her denials. It was rather like being in a net, thought Jenny despondently; she was aware that her friends at hospital had envied her; a lesser stately home to go to on her days off, money of her own, titled aunts and uncles, a nice young man waiting to marry her and transfer her to exactly the same kind of background. . .it was all so suitable, and yet she felt trapped. And now here was Aunt Bess positively pushing him at her!

To leave Aunt Bess to her own devices was unthinkable; she owed her a happy childhood and untold kindness; besides, she loved her irascible aunt. She would have to make the best of it, and once she was restored to health she would look for another job—and somehow she would have to convince Toby that she wasn't the wife for him. She had never given him any encouragement, but he still called each day, sometimes twice, always at the most inconvenient times, tagging along behind her while she arranged the flowers or polished the more valuable silver on display. Once or twice the Professor had seen them together, and for some reason that had annoyed her.

But she had fun too; Oliver was a delightful companion. They climbed trees, explored the wilder corners of the park while she taught him the names of the birds and small wild animals they encountered, fished for minnows in the stream which ran through the grounds, and fed the carp in the pond. And when she could spare the time, she took him round the house, pointing out its lovely furnishings and portraits, showing him the priest's hole and the cellars. The only place she wouldn't take him to was the top of the clock tower at the end of the south front.

'You'll have to wait,' she told him. 'There were a lot of starlings there this spring and it's full of old birds' nests. I must go up there and clear them away now the birds have gone.' And she had coaxed him to examine the glass case of family jewellery at the back of the hall instead.

It was a couple of days later when she found herself with an hour to spare before lunch. Armed with a broom and a sack, she took the unwieldy key from its hook behind the garden door and went to open the narrow arched door of the clock tower. There was no way in which to reach it from the house nowadays; the inside door had been walled up, and as the clock seldom needed attention, the outside door was enough. She climbed the narrow circular staircase quickly, not minding the musty smell and the dimness, and at the top produced a second key to open an even smaller door, and stepped into the square, stone-walled room which housed the clock. She had been right; the place was littered with old nests, feathers and all the debris of a large number of birds, and she set to work to clear it away. It took longer than she had expected and she had to hurry a little towards the end, dragging her full sack to the door and leaning it against the wall while she opened the door. It groaned and creaked as she went through and then shut behind her, and when she turned in a vain effort to keep it open in order to retrieve the sack, she dropped the key. She was bending to pick it up when the steps directly below her began to collapse slowly, tumbling down lazily, going out of sight round the angle of the winding stair. Jenny stood teetering on the top still, unable to believe her eyes, unable to go back—even if she had had the courage to move, for the key had tumbled with the steps—and certainly unable to go forward.

She took a long trembling breath and made herself think calmly while she clutched at the rough stones on either side of her. Panic she must not, that would be disaster, and shouting wouldn't help; there was the whole length of the south front between her and anyone likely to hear her voice. Perhaps when the ruin of steps below her had settled, she would be able to work her way down. She looked away from the still shifting rubble and tried to remember if she had told anyone where she was going, and concluded that she hadn't told a soul. Only at the back of her mind was the faint memory of having mentioned it to someone, but she couldn't remember who and even if she had it had probably not registered.

She was wrong. It had registered with Oliver, and when Miss Creed demanded that her niece should be fetched so that she might dance attendance upon her when the Professor called, and

Jenny was nowhere to be found, and nor had anyone seen her in the house or grounds for quite some time, he joined the group of grown-ups discussing her probable whereabouts, but no one paid attention to him; they were too busy explaining her absence to the Professor, who had just arrived. He was inclined to think nothing of it. 'Probably gone for a walk,' he offered laconically. 'Perhaps Margaret could stand in. . .?'

But Aunt Bess wasn't going to have Margaret. 'Pooh,' she declared loudly, 'the girl's no use at all. If Jenny can't be found, then you can go home again, and don't dare to charge me a fee!'

The Professor hid a grin and then looked down at Oliver, tugging gently at his sleeve. 'I think I know where Jenny is,' he told him. 'She told me she would have to clean the clock tower room—it's full of old birds' nests—she told me so.'

The Professor eyed him thoughtfully. 'Did she know that I was coming this morning?'

'Course she did. She went to do her hair again after breakfast and when I asked her why she said: "Well, the old Prof's coming, isn't he? and I want to look severe."' Oliver paused. 'Why?'

A smile tugged at the corner of the Professor's mouth. 'We must ask her, mustn't we? I'll go and fetch her.'

'Shall I come with you?'

The big man smiled again. 'I think not, Oliver.

Perhaps you would like to show me the carp later?'

He detached himself from the little group of people standing around and strolled off in the direction of the Clock Tower, along the south front, not hurrying in the least. The door was still open, he doubled himself up and went, still without haste, up the staircase.

Jenny heard the creak of the door and the unhurried steps and made herself look down from the spot on the wall where she had fastened her gaze because she was afraid of getting giddy. 'Don't come up,' she shouted in a not quite steady voice, 'the steps have crumbled.'

The footsteps didn't pause, and she shouted again urgently, 'For heaven's sake, listen!'

'I heard you very well the first time,' observed the Professor, rounding the last curve and stopping to contemplate the mass of masonry between them, 'but since I'm a humane man and unwilling to leave anyone, even you, in such a pickle, I considered it my duty to come and see what you were shouting about.'

Jenny choked back a strong desire to burst into tears. 'I'm glad you find it amusing,' she told him in an icy, shaking little voice. 'And now if you would be so good as to fetch someone—Florrie will know what to do. . .'

'Don't be silly,' he told her calmly, 'Florrie won't have the least idea what to do—besides, there's no need to fetch anyone—you only have to jump.'

'Jump?' uttered Jenny on a screech. 'It's ten feet—more. And where, pray, do I jump to?'

'Me.'

He was leaning back against the wall, poised in what she considered to be quite a dangerous manner on a pile of broken stones. He looked incapable of supporting himself, let alone her. 'No,' said Jenny.

'Afraid?'

'Well, of course I am—I'm scared stiff, if you must know. I'll stay here.'

'Which hardly solves our small problem. I'll count three and you'll jump.'

'I won't!'

'No pluck,' he observed to the opposite wall. 'Your illustrious ancestors would turn in their graves at your sad lack of courage.'

She said nastily: 'I don't suppose you've got any illustrious ancestors, but if you had, they must have disowned you years ago. . .ordering me about. . .'

He chuckled. 'My dear girl, come on. I'm getting cramp.'

'All the more reason why I should stay here.' Her hand slipped on the stones and she gasped with fright.

'You see? You only have to do that with both

hands at the same time. . .' His voice held mockery. 'Jump, Jenny.'

'I shall knock you down.'

He let out a crack of laughter. 'You're what?—eight stone?—less, maybe. Well, I'm over fifteen.' He went on in a matter-of-fact manner: 'Your aunt was very annoyed. I daresay that by now she's allowed herself to get into a towering rage, and you know how bad that can be for her.' He smiled suddenly. 'Come on, Jenny, even if you can't stand the sight of me, you can trust me.'

Which, when she thought about it, was true enough. She closed her eyes, made a funny, helpless little sound, and jumped.

It was like hitting a tree trunk and just as solid. She had landed fair and square on to the professor's waistcoat and his arms held her tight against it. She could hear the hurried beat of his heart under her ear and mumbled: 'We'll never be able to move from here,' as another stair crumbled slowly away.

'Rubbish—you do as I tell you and we'll be at the bottom in a matter of seconds. Loosen your strangle-hold a little.'

She withdrew her arms from his neck so sharply that she almost overbalanced. 'I said loosen it,' the Professor pointed out mildly. 'And now do exactly as I say—you can argue about it afterwards.' She felt his arms slacken and gave a little gasp and heard his: 'No—now, remember those ancestors. I'm going to grip you by the elbows and swing you clear of the next two steps—I don't fancy they'll bear even your weight. I'll hold you until you've found your feet, then you must hang on to the wall until I join you.'

She clutched his waistcoat for a few seconds. 'All right, I'm ready.'

She felt herself swung down in a gentle arc. 'Grab the wall, left hand first—now the right. Good girl, I'm going to let go now. I'll be with you in a moment.'

And he was, balancing his weight beside her before trying the step below. 'Come on,' he encouraged her, and gave her a hand to hold. 'Get a foot on this one, but don't stay on it—get on to the next one if you can.'

It was quite easy after that, only they had to take care not to be on the same stair together, and once or twice the Professor had to stride over them as they slid away under his weight. As they reached the bottom they could hear the staircase breaking up very slowly behind them. The Professor shut the door and locked it and put the key in his pocket. 'Just in case Oliver decides to have a look,' he explained, 'and now stand still while I dust you down.'

She stood meekly while he brushed the dust off her linen dress, then took his handkerchief and wiped her face and lastly shook out her mane of hair. She should have been able to do these things for herself, but she was shaking so much that she was incapable of it. When he had at length finished, she said in a voice which still shook a little. 'Thank you—thank you very much. I was very tiresome, wasn't I? I should have known better. I'm an awful coward.'

He smiled very kindly at her. 'If you had been a coward, you would still be there on the top step. Do you feel you can face your aunt, or do you want a breather?'

'I'm all right now, thank you. Are you? I didn't hurt you when I jumped?'

He was brushing dust off his sleeve. 'No.' He sounded, even in that one brief word, as though he were laughing. 'Shall we go, then?'

It was Margaret who came to meet them as they went into the house. 'Jenny, where have you been? Aunt Bess is so cross. How could you go away like that, you knew Eduard was coming?'

Eduard indeed! 'I got hung up—so sorry.' Jenny moved away from the Professor and started to cross the hall to the cloakroom cunningly hidden in the panelled wall. 'I'll tidy myself—I won't be a minute.'

The Professor was already with her aunt when she reached the room. He must have told her what had happened because she said at once: 'Janet, you will be good enough to get someone to see about the tower staircase—it must be replaced or rebuilt. You're all right?' a little belatedly.

'Perfectly, thank you, Aunt Bess.'

'Humph—I hope you're grateful to Eduard.'
She didn't look at him. 'Yes, I am.'

'Fetch the brochure of that cruise I intend to go on.' Aunt Bess waved a beringed hand and turned to the Professor. 'It seems comfortable enough—I have arranged for us to have cabins on the sun deck. It will be quiet there, and any meals I wish to take there will be brought to me. I've made the ship's agent fully conversant with my state of health.'

'You have been busy.' The Professor's tone was dry.

'Well, Jenny has arranged it all, of course, she's good at that sort of thing. There is a doctor on board as well as a nurse—not that I shall need the latter. Jenny will look after me.'

'She has given up her post at Queen's?' he queried softly.

'Naturally.' Miss Creed shot him a suspicious look. 'I have never approved of her taking up nursing, especially at that hospital in the East End.'

'But if she had not trained as a nurse, you wouldn't have had her services now, Miss Creed.'

'That is beside the point,' said Aunt Bess grandly. 'She will be having a delightful holiday.'

'And afterwards?'

She stared at him and he looked back at her with a bland face.

'I'm sure I don't know—probably she'll marry. It's high time she did.'

Jenny had very little time to regret leaving Queen's. Aunt Bess, getting stronger every day, kept her busy with plans and arrangements for their cruise as well as overhauling her extensive wardrobe. And Jenny went to London and bought some new clothes for herself too—cool cottons and sundresses and several pretty evening dresses. She spent two days there, staying with one of her friends from Queen's, listening with nostalgia to the hospital gossip, and then driving back to Dimworth the next day, just in time to take her share of looking after the visitors to the house after she had given an account of her brief trip to Aunt Bess.

It was a lovely day and there were more people than usual. She was tired and hot by teatime, and the sight of Margaret, cool and serene, strolling in the rose garden with the Professor in tow did nothing to improve her mood. Margaret had a generous allowance from the estate and was free to regard it as her home should she wish to do so, but she made no effort to take her part in maintaining it. Indeed, when she came to stay, she expected that the whole place should be geared to her wishes, never mind how inconvenient it was, and even Aunt Bess's illness hadn't been allowed to spoil her gentle, selfish routine. As for little Oliver, he was left to his own devices, and if it hadn't been for Jenny, he would have had little enough fun.

Jenny, watching his mother sink gracefully on to a rustic seat, wondered how he would fare while she was away. Margaret had said that she would remain at Dimworth provided she wasn't expected to have anything to do with the visitors, which meant that Jenny had had to tour round the estate seeking helpers to fill in with the polishing of the furniture and silver, selling of postcards and the like, and carry on with all the small chores she attended to herself when she was at Dimworth. She took a last look at the pair, Margaret leaning back against the seat as though she were exhausted, and the Professor standing there, looking at her. 'Silly fool,' muttered Jenny, and sped away to make sure that the first batch of visitors hadn't strayed through any of the doors marked private.

She had crossed the hall and was deliberating as to whether she should go and find Mrs Thorpe or make sure that the collection of dolls was properly arranged, when the Professor, with the suddenness of someone who had popped up out of the ground at her feet, was beside her.

She looked at him with some interest. 'That was prettty smartish,' she observed. 'Did you run all the way? And how did you know. . .?'

'I saw you looking at us, and when you flounced off in that fashion I thought I'd better come after you and find out what had annoyed you this time.'

She had decided on the dolls and was already walking rapidly towards the tables where they were displayed. 'You always make me out to be bad tempered,' she snapped crossly, 'and I didn't flounce. And I'm not in the least annoyed.'

She twitched a wax doll's muslin skirt to exactness moved a baby doll carefully an inch to the left and stood back, her head on one side, refusing to look at him.

'Looking forward to your holiday?' His voice was friendly.

'Yes—no—I really haven't had the time to think about it—I have a lot to do.'

'While Margaret strolls in the rose garden.' He had spoken softly, but Jenny went a fiery red under his little smile.

She said stiffly: 'This is Oliver's home and Margaret is his mother, when she is here she naturally does exactly as she likes, and why shouldn't she?'

'Oh, quite. Only it seems to me that you don't always do exactly as you would like, Jenny.'

He sounded so kind and understanding that she found herself saying: 'Ah, yes, but you see it's a different kettle of fish with me. Aunt Bess has looked after me all my life, or most of it—and

Dimworth has been my home. Margaret is quite entitled to tell me to leave, but she's too kind.' Too lazy to bother, too, she added silently.

'A charming person,' murmured the Professor. 'I'm sure she wouldn't do anything so unkind. Besides if you went away, someone else would have to be found to fill your place; dust and polish and run errands and keep an eye on the visitors and entertain Oliver while he is here.'

'I like doing it,' said Jenny sharply.

'You had a very promising career, so Doctor Toms was telling me.'

'That's none of your business.' She began to march back the way she had come. 'I have to find Mrs Thorpe.'

'In that cupboard place behind the hall where you keep the brochures. And it might be my business, Jenny.'

She stopped short to look at him. Was he serious about Margaret? Was he actually going to marry her? It would be nice for Oliver. She said quickly: Margaret is lovely and very sweet— she's been lonely since big Oliver died.'

She dived into the little room to confer with Mrs Thorpe without seeing the expression on the Professor's face.

She hardly spoke to him again before she and Aunt Bess left; true, he called to see her aunt and exchanged a few commonplace remarks to her concerning that lady's care while they were away, and although Jenny longed to ask him how long he planned to stay with Doctor Toms, she didn't do so.

Sitting beside Aunt Bess in the vintage Vauxhall Miss Creed refused to part with, being driven up to the docks at Tilbury to join their ship, she reflected that even after these weeks of seeing him almost every day, she still didn't know anything about him, only that he wasn't married and lived and worked in Holland. She wondered if Aunt Bess knew, but it was hardly the time to ask for her companion was resting with her eyes closed. Jenny looked at the elderly face with real affection; Aunt Bess was an old tartar, but a delightful one, with plenty of courage, determined at all costs that after her change of scene, she would return to Dimworth and take up the reins once more as though she had never had to relinquish them.

The ship was smallish and carried no more than three hundred passengers; moreover it was well appointed, with plenty of space. Their cabins on the sun-deck were all that could be desired, side by side well furnished and each with a bathroom. Jenny saw her aunt settled, summoned the stewardess to unpack for her, and retired to her own cabin, where she was presently visited by the purser with the news that they were to sit at the captain's table and that the ship's doctor would call upon them very shortly. They had only to ask for anything they required, he added. She thanked him warmly, unpacked, arranged her hair to her satisfaction, added a little more lipstick and went back to her aunt, who expressed satisfaction at the purser's message, gave it her opinion that her surroundings would do very well, and ordered tea.

The ship had set sail before they had finished and Jenny composed her aunt for a nap before going on deck to have a look round. In rather less than five minutes she was encircled by an eager little group of men, only too glad to explain just what the ship was doing and why. She treated them all with impartial kindness, refused a variety of invitations to have a drink, dance after dinner, explore the ship and try out the swimming pool in the morning with equal pleasantness, made her excuses charmingly and went off to the wireless room to send a message to Dimworth. She had promised Oliver that the moment they set sail she would let him know, and she remembered now how wistful he had looked when she had kissed him goodbye.

Something would have to be done about him; of course, if the Professor intended to marry Margaret, that would be splendid for Oliver, for he and the boy liked each other, but just supposing that didn't happen? The little boy had several years of loneliness before he would be sent to school; his grandparents in Scotland were delightful people, but hardly of an age to be his companions, and Margaret was of no use at all. He had one or two friends among the game-keepers' children who lived close by there, but although they might be good friends for him, their language sometimes left a lot to be desired and Oliver, like all small boys, had picked up the worst of it with all the ease in the world.

She sent her message and wandered back to her cabin; they were to have dinner there on their first evening, so that Aunt Bess might go to bed early after her long journey by car. It was still only nine o'clock by the time Jenny had helped her aunt to bed, saw to it that she had everything she might need for the night, and gone to her own cabin once more. She would have liked to have gone on deck, but she had already refused to join in the evening's activities. She undressed slowly, got into bed and opened her book, turning its pages without taking in a word for the niggling thought at the back of her mind that she hadn't said goodbye to the Professor quite distracted her. She flung the book down presently and turned out the light. After all, he could have taken the trouble to find her himself if he had wanted to couldn't he? Only he hadn't.

But she had no intention of allowing such a small—figuratively speaking, of course—thing as the Professor spoil the cruise. Subject to Aunt Bess vagaries, she joined in the deck games,

danced every evening with a great variety of partners, sunbathed on deck in the increasing warmth,
and tried her hand at the fruit machines. But not
always; Aunt Bess took her place at the captain's
table at lunch and dinner and had her own special
corner in one of the bars before these meals, to
which a select few were invited to join her, but
she retired early and had her breakfast in bed,
and moreover, liked Jenny to read to her while
she rested in the afternoons, so that Jenny's time
wasn't quite her own. Not that she complained,
even to herself; they had come on the cruise for
the benefit of her aunt's health, and that should
come first.

All the same, she found herself looking forward
to their arrival at Madeira. Aunt Bess had already
decided that she wouldn't go ashore, but Jenny
could if she wished; just for an hour or so in the
morning before the ship sailed for Lanzarote.

They docked early in the morning and Jenny
slipped on deck to get her first sight of Funchal,
its white houses lining the water's edge and
climbing into the mountains looming at its back.
It looked lovely in the early morning light; she
craned her neck in all directions to get a better
view and went back to drink her tea and dress
before going to see how Aunt Bess was. She had
had a good night, she declared, but still had no
desire to go ashore. 'On the way back,' she
decided, 'but if you see anything you fancy,

Jenny, buy it—the embroidery is exquisite, you
know—something for Margaret and handker-
chiefs for Mrs Thorpe, I suppose. Get what you
like. . .' She pushed her tray aside. 'And get me
a paper, child, will you? Now run along and have
your breakfast and go ashore, but be certain to
be back in good time.'

'You don't mind?' asked Jenny anxiously.
'You'll be all right? I've told the doctor. . .'

'Don't fuss!'

Jenny skipped away to eat an excellent breakfast, count her *escudos* and leave the ship. It had
been a little difficult to avoid the offers of company she had received, for she hadn't felt
sociable, but by dint of hanging about until almost
everyone had gone ashore, she had succeeded,
although she had been delayed at the last minute
by a cablegram from Toby, asking her if she had
changed her mind. Without stopping to think she
had gone back to Aunt Bess and spoken her mind,
scowling horribly as she tore it up and flung it
into the wastepaper basket, and Aunt Bess had
said sharply: 'You're being a silly girl, Janet. It
would be an excellent marriage from every point
of view.'

'Except mine,' snorted Jenny.

'Pooh!' her aunt had spoken strongly. 'You
don't know what you want.'

Jenny wandered down the gangway after that,
smiled at the first officer who was standing on

the quay, and strolled through the noise and bustle around her, looking cool and very pretty in her blue cotton dress and wide straw hat. Perhaps she didn't know what she wanted, she mused, but at least she knew what she didn't want. She walked on, out of the dock and along the road towards the town. It was already warm and she had no definite plans of what she should do. A little shopping, she supposed, and a long, cool drink in a café.

CHAPTER FIVE

SHE had been walking for perhaps five minutes when she saw the Professor strolling towards her, nattily dressed in light slacks and a cotton shirt. She almost fell over her own feet, stopping so suddenly at the sight of him, aware of a glow of pleasure flooding her person, which, considering that they didn't like other, seemed strange.

His, 'Good morning, Jenny Wren,' was coolly friendly and showed no surprise.

'Well, I never!' she exclaimed. 'However did you get here?'

He forbore from telling her that he had flown his own plane over. 'Oh, there are ways and means,' he told her airily.

'Oh—on holiday?' she went on.

'Er—yes, one might call it that. Your aunt is on board?'

'Yes. Were you going to see her? I left her writing letters. . .'

'You have had your breakfast?'

'Ages ago.'

Would it annoy you very much to come with me while I look her over?' He caught her by the arm and turned her round smartly and began to

stroll back towards the quayside, without waiting
for her reply. I remembered that your ship would
be calling here this morning and it seemed a suitable opportunity. . .'

'You aren't worried about her?' asked Jenny
quickly.

'If you mean do I anticipate any recurrence of
the old trouble, I do not.' He went on to talk
about nothing much until they reached the ship
once more. As they went past the first officer,
Jenny paused to explain: 'My aunt's doctor,' and
when they were out of earshot:

'My dear girl,' observed her companion mildly.
'I'm a surgeon. You, a nurse, should know the
difference.'

'Well, of course I do,' she was a little
impatient. 'I didn't know you were so fussy about
a little thing like that.'

The Professor made a small choking sound.
'There is a considerable difference—' he began,
still mild to be cut short by her: 'Oh, don't be so
stuffy!'

They had reached the sun-deck by now and
she tapped on her aunt's door, looking at him
over her shoulder as she spoke.

He swooped, there was no other word for it,
and kissed her hard and with expertise. 'Stuffy?'
he asked silkily, and hearing Miss Creed's voice
bidding them enter, opened the door. Jenny
stepped past him nicely pink in the cheeks, her

chin up, her eyes very bright, so that Aunt Bess, looking up from her writing, exclaimed tartly: 'You look as though you've been quarrelling or kissing, Janet—which. . .' She paused as her eyes lighted on the Professor's vast frame in the doorway. 'Ah, it's you.' She didn't sound surprised. 'And are you on holiday too, Eduard?'

Despite her sharp voice she smiled at him and his mouth curved a little as he told her: 'A brief day or so. I realised that you would be calling here today and it seemed a good idea to look you up.'

'Huh—to examine me, I suppose, and send me a bill afterwards.'

'Er—examine you, yes, but since we are both on holiday I had intended to waive my fee.'

Miss Creed took him up smartly. 'You're more sensible than I thought. Certainly you may examine me. Now?'

'If it is convenient,' he murmured, 'and just a few questions. . .'

His patient threw down her book. 'Jenny, turn yourself into a nurse and see to me.' And to the Professor: 'Where is your stethoscope?'

'I hardly think I need it. Your pulse, a quick look at the scar, and as I said, a question or two.'

Miss Creed waved an imperious hand at Jenny. Then run along, child, I shan't need you. Be back for lunch.'

But Jenny stayed where she was. 'You don't

need me, Professor van Draak?' she asked in a cool voice. His glance was quick and casual. 'Not at the moment, thank you.'

'Then be sure and return at the right time,' reiterated her aunt, and since there was nothing more to be said, she went.

But somehow the fun had gone out of the morning. She walked slowly away from the ship and along the road curving beside the water until she reached the town, where she pottered a little aimlessly round the shops, had a long, cool drink at a pavement café, quite unconscious of the stares her pretty face and bright hair induced, and then wandered on again. She was supposed to be buying things, but it was getting warm now and although she had an hour to kill, she felt disinclined to spend it in the shops.

The small side streets looked inviting and a little mysterious, leading away from the town's centre towards the mountains looming in the distance. Jenny turned into one of them and had taken barely a dozen paces when the Professor's large, firm hand gripped her shoulder, making her jump and turn sharply.

'Not up here, dear girl,' he begged her.

'Scaring me like that!' uttered Jenny peevishly. 'Creeping up behind me. . .'

'I didn't creep.' He sounded meek, although she was sure that he wasn't meek at all. 'I merely followed you to warn you that this part of the town isn't really for young tourists.'

'Who is it for?'

His eyes laughed down at her. 'Shall we say men only?'

She gave him a stony look. 'Well, there's no way of knowing.' She felt belligerent, caught unawares, and at a disadvantage.

His hand slid from her shoulder and caught her elbow instead and she found herself walking back the way she had come. 'I should have been perfectly all right,' she protested with slight pettishness.

He stopped to look down at her. 'With that face and hair?' He shook his head. 'Come and have a drink.'

'I've had one, thank you.'

'One should drink plenty in this heat. Doctor's advice.'

'But you're not a doctor—you're a surgeon, you said so.'

'Ah, yes—so I did. I'm a modest man; I tend to hide my light under a bushel. I do happen to be a doctor of medicine, but I never cared for the medical side and I tend to forget. . .'

'Well,' said Jenny, exasperated, 'you might have told me!'

'You didn't ask.' He had steered her through the streets to a pavement table outside one of the cafés and pulled out a chair. 'Now sit down and bury the hatchet while you cool your fiery feel-

ings with a long drink. What would you like?
Have you tried Sangria?'

'No—I had a soft drink.'

'Then you must sample it.' He sat down
gingerly on the flimsy chair and gave their order,
then went on chattily: 'So pleasant, these brief
interludes.'

She let that pass. 'How did you find Aunt Bess?
Better, I hope?' She wasn't going to give him
the satisfaction of admitting that she found them
pleasant too.

He waited until their drinks arrived. 'Remark-
ably fit—good reactions, and provided that she
has told me the truth, she is making excellent
progress. She will never be quite one hundred per
cent again, you know that, but provided that she's
moderately careful she should be able to resume
a more or less normal life. Do you mind if
I smoke?'

Jenny said that no she didn't and watched him
fill his pipe. When it was nicely alight he asked:
'I take it there will be a good chance of you going
back to your job?'

She shook her head. 'Not at Queen's and not
for some time, I think. You see, Dimworth is
quite a large place to manage. But the season will
be over soon; if Aunt Bess feels quite fit by then,
I'll see about getting another job.'

'You mind giving up your nursing?'

She sipped her drink and found it good. 'Well,

yes—you see, while I'm in hospital I'm independent.'

'And when you're at Dimworth you have to conform?'

She had forgotten that she didn't like him, that he was arrogant and brusque and laughed at her. Just to voice her troubled thoughts was a relief, and he was easy to talk to. 'Yes.'

'And dwindle away into spinsterhood? I think not.'

'Well, no—actually Aunt Bess wants me to marry. . .'

'She has mentioned it—the young man Toby. Very suitable, I gather.'

'Yes, but I don't want to marry him.' She sounded pathetic without meaning to.

'This is a free world, Jenny—or at least parts of it are, and it's your life, isn't it? Throw him over, this so worthy young man.'

'Well, I've been throwing him over for years—but he's so—so nice—much too nice for me.'

'You wish to marry a man who is not nice?' There was laughter in his voice.

'Don't pick on words!' snapped Jenny. 'You know very well what I mean.' She sucked her drink throught the two straws with childlike pleasure and went on. 'He's—he's. . .well, if you must know, he always lets me have my own way.'

Her companion puffed smoke gently, his eyes on the graceful rings he was making. 'Ah—and you are wise enough to know that wouldn't be a good thing for you.'

'I never. . .' began Jenny. 'He's a very nice man, I said so.' She added unkindly: 'He's young too.'

The Professor looked blandly across the little table at her. 'Another reason why you shouldn't marry him—although,' he went on judicially, 'perhaps you would suit each other very well after all. You could be bossy-boots for the rest of your life and he would become nicer and nicer—meek is I think your word for it. Your children would be simply ghastly.'

Jenny choked. 'Bossy-boots!' she exclaimed. Whatever next?' She swallowed the rest of her drink, anxious to be gone from this tiresome man. 'I am not—and my children will be simply super. . .'

'Given the right father,' conceded the Professor, and Jenny, choking again on the last few drops of her drink, caught her breath and had to be slapped sharply on the back, so that the tears stood in her eyes and she became quite purple in the face.

'You really shouldn't allow yourself to become so worked up,' advised the Professor kindly, 'nor should you gobble down your drinks in that fashion.'

Jenny, her breath back, let it out slowly. 'You are quite detestable,' she told him in an icy voice unfortunately spoilt by a hiccough. 'I am not worked up, only when you deliberately annoy me.'

'My dear Miss Wren—or may I call you Jenny?—I am the mildest of men. . .'

'Rubbish, and you've been calling me Jenny for goodness knows how long. You are a bad-tempered man, determined to annoy me!'

His look of astonishment was a masterpiece. 'Good gracious—I? Annoy you? Though I must confess to a bad temper. A man must have a few faults,' he added modestly. 'Have another Sangria?'

She said with dignity, 'Very well, I will, thank you.'

He beamed at her. 'Friends again?' He didn't wait for her to answer but embarked upon a gentle flow of small talk which required little or no answer. Indeed, he gave her very little chance of replying even if she had wanted to, and at length interrupted himself to say: 'It's almost lunch time, I'll take you back to the ship.'

They went by taxi, and Jenny was unaccountably annoyed at his very casual goodbye at the foot of the gangplank.

She lunched with little appetite and then, because Aunt Bess had changed her mind and wanted to go ashore after all, spent the next hour or so in a hired car which took them from Funchal along the coast road to Canico and Santa Cruz and Machico, before driving over the Portela Pass to Faial. Aunt Bess was getting tired by then, so they stopped for a cool drink and returned to the ship in plenty of time to settle her for a nap before dressing for dinner. She was already dozing as Jenny left her and went to her own cabin to review her wardrobe. There were several pretty dresses she hadn't worn yet, but she eyed them without much interest; any old thing would do, she decided for there was no one to notice what she wore. She didn't go too deeply into who the no one might be and perhaps in defiance of the half hidden thought, made up her mind to make the effort after all and wear a leaf green chiffon, a filmy creation which looked nothing at all on its hanger but did wonders for a girl once it was on, especially when she happened to have coppery hair.

Aunt Bess, refreshed after her nap, and with the stewardess to help her, and clothed herself with some splendour, zipped and buttoned into plum-coloured silk, a number of gold chains draped across her massive front. She lifted the old-fashioned gold-rimmed spectacles hanging from one of them as Jenny went in and studied her niece.

'Very nice,' she pronounced. 'We will have a drink.'

Tonic water, Aunt,' said Jenny firmly, and led her elderly relative to the nearest lift.

The bar was quite full; Jenny knew most of the people there by now and she smiled and nodded to them as she accompanied her aunt to their usual corner, left empty by tacit consent. Only it wasn't empty. The Professor, in all the subdued elegance of white dinner jacket and black tie, was already there. He rose and came towards them and took Miss Creed's hand. 'This is delightful,' he observed, addressing her and smiling only briefly at Jenny. 'I've taken the liberty of ordering your usual drinks.'

He had settled Aunt Bess in her usual seat as he spoke, pulled out a chair for Jenny and sat down between them before she found her voice to say: 'Are you travelling on this ship too? I thought. . .'

His smile held a touch of mockery and his voice was cool. 'You forget, I'm on holiday too.'

She persisted: 'Yes, but this morning. . .'

'I don't remember it being mentioned,' he snubbed her gently, and turned to make small talk with Miss Creed while Jenny, in a quite nasty temper, studied his profile. Arrogant, she muttered silently, and rude he could at least pretend to be civil! She stared at the glass in her hand, gloomily contemplating several days of avoiding his company. His quiet observation, 'Yes, it is quite a small ship as ships go,' was so appropriate to her thoughts that she flushed and drank unwisely, almost all of her Pimm's Number One.

It didn't help at all, either, when he leaned forward and took the glass from her hand and said in an avuncular manner: 'I did warn you not to gobble your drinks, Jenny.'

She shot him a fiery look, quite unable to answer for the moment, and in any case Aunt Bess had embarked on an account of their afternoon drive in her compelling voice, allowing for no one else to speak save when she paused for suitable comment.

The Professor was sitting at the captain's table too. What was worse, he faced Jenny across it, so that each time she looked up, it was to find his eyes upon her, a fact which caused her to carry on an animated conversation with the elderly man on her right—something to do with shipping, although she wasn't sure what—and presently she turned her attention to the famous journalist on her left, whose manner was a shade too charming for her taste. Until now she had kept him at arm's length, but now, with the Professor within a yard or so of her, his firm mouth curled into the tiniest of sneers, she allowed herself to be drawn into frivolous chat with the man. But before long she wished that she hadn't been so forthcoming, for he showed every sign of turning the inch she had given him into an ell. Moreover, she was only too well aware of the Professor's sardonic eye. She was doing her best to wriggle gracefully out of accepting an invitation to go on a sightseeing tour of Lanzarote in the journalist's hired car when the Professor came to her rescue.

'What a delightful prospect,' he murmured across the table, 'but aren't you forgetting that your aunt will need you while she has that treatment we have decided to try?'

Jenny was too grateful to express surprise at this piece of information—indeed, she admired the Professor for the convincing way he had spoken. Her 'Oh, dear—I'd quite forgotten, thank you for reminding me, Professor van Draak,' was a masterpiece of regret.

Aunt Bess wanted to go to her cabin directly after dinner, and Jenny went with her. It was still early and there would be dancing until the small hours, but Aunt Bess, after a leisurely half hour of undressing, had other ideas. 'You shall read to me, Jenny,' she decreed. 'You have a pretty voice and I find it soothing. The editorial in the *Guardian*, I think.'

So Jenny read. She read for a couple of hours and even then her aunt demanded that she should sit with her until she fell asleep, and by the time she had done that Jenny was too tired herself to join the captain and his party in one of the lounges, and certainly too tired to dance.

She didn't see anything of the Professor until lunch-time the next day, when he appeared at the table, wished his companions a good day and applied himself to the task of entertaining Miss

Creed. It wasn't until that lady was being escorted to her cabin for her post-prandial nap that Jenny had the opportunity to ask: 'What treatment?'

The Professor, who had attached himself to them waved an airy hand. 'Purely mythical, Jenny, purely mythical. You were so completely bogged down, were you not? Only the unkindest of men would have left you in such a predicament.'

He opened Miss Creed's door so that both ladies might enter and Jenny edged past him without speaking. 'Ungrateful girl,' he murmured into the top of head, and shut the door silently behind them. It had barely closed when Aunt Bess exclaimed: 'My scarf—I left it in the restaurant.'

'Well, you don't need it at present,' said Jenny reasonably. 'I'll fetch it later.'

'I require it now. I refuse to take my nap until I have it.'

Jenny sighed, muttered under her breath and started back to the restaurant, to find her way barred by the Professor, lounging at the end of the corridor.

'You disposed of your aunt very quickly.'

She shot him a cross look. 'I haven't—she left her scarf in the restaurant, and she wants it this minute.'

'Do I detect a slight vexation? Where is your sunny disposition, Jenny Wren? Snappish, and no gratitude for your rescue, either.'

She made an effort to work her way round him. 'Well, I haven't had the time. . .'

'To express your deep obligation to me? But this will take very little time, my dear.'

He had kissed her soundly before she could dodge him and then disconcerted her utterly by standing aside without another word, to let her pass.

She lingered unnecessarily in the restaurant so that he would be gone by the time she went back, and was quite put out to find that that was exactly what he had done.

The ship had been delayed at Madeira, but now Lanzarote was clearly visible ahead of them. Jenny looked longingly at its mountains as she went back to her aunt's cabin, for she saw little chance of going ashore. They were due to sail again in the evening and although there was a coachload of passengers going on an afternoon tour, Aunt Bess had refused to consider staying quietly on board while Jenny joined them. She went into the cabin, handed over the scarf, picked up various articles Aunt Bess had dropped and prepared to go again, to be halted at the door by her aunt's voice. 'I understand the island is very interesting—Eduard has offered to drive you round this afternoon. I told him that you would be delighted.'

'Aunt Bess, I'm not a child—I can accept my own invitations, and the Professor hasn't said anything to me. In any case, I don't want to go, thank you—I'd much rather go with the coach.'

'Out of the question, Janet.'

'I've just told you I'm not a child!'

'You're behaving like one. I thought it very kind of Eduard. He pointed out that the coach will be hot and stuffy and probably break down. But if you won't go, you'd better go and tell him so now—he's on this deck, up in the bows.'

'Oh, Aunt Bess. . .!' Jenny shut the door quietly behind her, although she wanted very much to bang it. Aunt Bess meant it kindly, but why couldn't she stop interfering? Jenny went slowly out on to the deck, filled now with passengers watching the picturesque little town of Puerto de los Marmoles getting closer and closer. The Professor was standing with a number of other people, and she joined them silently, wondering how she was going to refuse his invitation without everyone around them hearing it too. There were two very pretty girls in the group, and either of them, from the way they were looking at him, would be only too delighted to take her place.

But it seemed that neither of them were to have that pleasure; he extricated himself from his companions with finesse, caught her by the arm and walked her briskly away.

'I have a car waiting,' he told her blandly. 'We

should have two or three hours in which to see something of the island.'

'I don't want. . .' began Jenny, and then changed it to: 'Well, it's awfully kind of you, but Aunt Bess. . .'

He nipped this in the bud. 'She assured me that you wanted to go ashore and that she wanted a few hours' rest and quiet. Ah, they're tying up now—you'll need a bonnet or something. I'll wait here.'

She saw that it was useless to protest, for he would either not hear or ride roughshod over any excuse she might be able to think up—and she couldn't think of any not without being rude.

In her cabin, searching for a pretty headscarf to go with her white cotton sun-dress, she toyed with the idea of staying there, only to discard it at once; to waste a glorious afternoon sitting alone when she could be exploring the island was just plain stupid. She arranged the scarf becomingly, put on a little more lipstick, and went back on deck.

The car was a small Citroën and rather battered, although it quickly proved its worth, for the Professor didn't linger in the town but made for the mountains towering to the north of the island. The road was a narrow one, but the surface was good, and he, who seemed to know his terrain, pointed out anything which he considered she might be interested in—dragon trees, the house

built by Omar Sharif when he had filmed on the
island some years previously, the once lived-in
caves. . .

'It's like the moon,' declared Jenny, 'and
there's no grass.'

'None at all—and you're right, it's so like the
moon that the astronauts came here to train before
their landing on the moon.'

She looked at him in surprise. 'However do
you know all these things?' she wanted to know.

He looked suitably modest. 'Oh, I pick up this
and that you know.'

They were climbing now, with mountains on
either side of them and now and again a glimpse
of the sea. It made a nice change of scenery when
they reached Teguise, a sleepy town with an old
Spanish style church in its square. But they didn't
stop, climbing on towards the northern coast
through the lava-strewn country, only slowing to
look briefly at the village of Haria; white-walled,
red-roofed houses and villas with colourful
gardens and surrounded by palm trees and giant
cactus.

'Well, that was nice,' observed Jenny, craning
her neck to get a last glimpse of the pretty
little place.

'There's something even nicer ahead of us.'

There was—right on the northern most coast
and atop a steep mountain slope which Jenny
privately thought the car wouldn't manage. The

Professor parked in the clearing at the top and whisked her out to lead her through a door in the high lava wall surrounding them. It opened into a wide, white washed passage leading to a cave, converted to a restaurant, but he took no notice of the tables and chairs but led her to the enormous plate glass window at the end so that she could admire the view from it—a sheer drop to the sea below, and separated from the mainland by a small stretch of water, a fair-sized island, its only village facing them.

'No electricity, no gas, no telephone, no shops,' explained the Professor, 'just a fishing village—a quiet paradise, although I believe it's popular in the season. Nice if you want to be alone. Come and have a drink.'

Jenny elected to have tea—hot water, a tea-bag and no milk, but it was refreshing. Her companion settled for coffee and while he drank it, regaled her with odds and ends of information about their surroundings.

'You know an awful lot about it,' she said. 'Have you been here before?'

'Twice—no, three times. It makes a nice change from the Dutch climate.'

Here was a chance to find out something about his home there. 'Do you live in a very cold part of the country?'

'It can be cold in the winter. If you've finished

we'll go,' he glanced at his watch. 'We'll take the coast road.'

She felt inward relief; she wasn't all that keen on mountains, and to be at sea level would suit her nicely. But it took a little while to get there; down the side of a mountain, along a narrow road full of hair-raising bends. It wouldn't have been so bad if the Professor had driven at a decorous pace, but it seemed to make no difference to him whether he was going up or down hill or on the flat; his pace was fast. They were within sight of the level road below them when he glanced at her briefly and said airily: 'Nervous? No need, I've been driving for years and I know this road. You look quite pale—where's your British phlegm, Jenny?'

'Thank you, it's still intact. I'm scared and I dare-say I'm as white as a sheet, but I have no intention of letting you have the satisfaction of frightening me. Pray go as fast as you like if that pleases your odious sense of humour.'

He laughed then and slowed down at once to a sedate pace. 'You don't like me at all, do you? Ever since we met and you tried to make me join the first batch of sightseers.'

She remembered how curt he had been. 'You were pompous.'

'Heaven forbid—but there, one is always prepared to think the worst of people one dislikes. This is the the bend.'

They were out on the coast road now, with the sea not far away. It ran between sand and rock, with here and there a small village and isolated villas with carefully cultivated gardens. There was a camel, too, working in the sand with a diminutive donkey beside it, and the Professor obligingly stopped so that Jenny might look her fill. And soon after that they were back in the town, threading its narrow streets, picturesque and colourful, spoilt by glimpses of poverty almost out of sight. And then they were outside the town again, passing the heaps of salt on the flat fields near the water, speeding towards the ship. The Professor drew up neatly before the gangway, ushered her out and prepared to pay the man waiting while Jenny strolled over to the small stalls set up on the quayside, laden with souvenirs. She hadn't meant to buy anything, but the vendors looked so eager that she had purchased postcards, several rush mats and an embroidered traycloth before the Professor rejoined her, paid for them, bade her buy no more and walked her briskly on board.

'You're too softhearted,' he told her severely.

She stopped in the ship's vestibule, empty for the moment. 'Thank you for the trip,' she said coldly, 'and if you will let me know how much you paid for these things, I'll let you have the money.' She suddenly felt cross with him. 'And I'm not softhearted—why shouldn't one help someone poorer than oneself? A few pesetas to them may make all the difference between meat or no meat for their dinner. She glared at him. 'The trouble is with you that you've got everything. . .'

He gave her a long thoughtful look and then without saying anything at all, turned on his heel and walked away from her.

There was nothing to do but to go to her aunt's cabin then, and that lady's crisp: 'You've been a long time, and in none too good a mood, I see?' did nothing to improve her temper. Luckily she didn't need to answer, for her aunt went on: 'Help me into my dress, child—we might go on deck for an hour before we change.'

Aunt Bess had her own corner with a chair always ready for her use; she reclined in it now, while Jenny gave a reluctant account of her afternoon, leaving out a great deal, so that presently her listener yawned, remarked that it sounded exceedingly dull and she would read for a while so that Jenny might do as she wished.

Thus dismissed, Jenny sauntered off to watch shuffleboard, hang over the side of the ship with several of her acquaintances and presently go with them to the bar by the swimming pool, where the younger passengers had formed the habit of gathering in the early evening. She stayed some time, sipping a long drink and pretending to herself that she wasn't keeping an eye open for the

Professor. There was no sign of him. He had disappeared like a puff of smoke, which, considering his size, seemed unlikely. All the same, when she went to dress for the evening she did so with extra care, piling her copper hair into thick coils on top of her head and zipping herself into a rather lovely pink chiffon which she had been keeping for a special occasion, telling herself that she might just as well wear it as allow it to hang in the cupboard.

She had barely installed her aunt in her usual corner by the bar when the Professor joined them, a steward at his elbow with their drinks. He greeted Aunt Bess warmly and Jenny in an offhand manner which made her grit her teeth, so that she said impulsively: 'Oh, hullo—I thought you'd jumped overboard.' She could have bitten her tongue out the moment she had uttered the words, for the look he gave her was amused and mocking too.

'You missed me?' he wanted to know blandly.

'No.' That didn't seem quite enough of an answer, so she added: 'I just happened to notice that you weren't around.' She picked up her glass and then put it down again; it would be just her luck to choke and have her back patronisingly patted.

'You don't like your drink?' he asked solicitously 'Let me get you something else.'

She snatched the glass up again, said: 'This is

fine thanks,' and sipped cautiously, thankful when Aunt Bess took the conversation into her own hands, as she almost always did.

It was as they were on their way in to dinner that the Professor managed to separate her from her aunt for long enough to murmur: 'Such a pretty girl this evening, and so very cross. Seasick, perhaps?'

She spoke rather wildly. 'Of course I'm not—cross or seasick.'

'In that case I'm sure Miss Creed will spare you after dinner for a little gentle exercise—dancing.'

Jenny had her mouth open to say no, but Aunt Bess, whose ears were still much too sharp, said loudly: 'A splendid idea. I shall watch.'

He danced very well indeed, although his hold was as impersonal as a kindly-natured man's might be on an elderly aunt he wished to indulge. Jenny, ruffled in her feelings, was wickedly delighted when the slow foxtrot gave way to something more modern; he wouldn't know what to do. . .

But he did—better than most of the other men in the room. She twisted and twirled, but so did he, with the unselfconscious manner of someone who had done it a hundred times already and wasn't afraid of making a fool of himself. When they rejoined their party, Aunt Bess paused long enough in her conversation with the captain to remark: 'If I were half my age, I should enjoy all that gyrating.' She waved a hand in regal dismissal. 'Go away and do it again—I'm not ready for bed yet.'

Before she went to sleep that night, Jenny, reviewing her evening, decided that if the Professor should ask her to drive round Tenerife with him, she would accept. True, he annoyed her almost all the time, but he drove superbly. There would be Las Palmas too. . . She closed her eyes, thinking sleepily that the cruise was quite fun after all. They would reach Tenerife quite early in the morning; she must be sure and be up early.

CHAPTER SIX

JENNY and Aunt Bess had breakfasted in the latter's cabin and the first coachload of sightseers were leaving the ship. There had been no sign of the Professor. Jenny had combed the ship without success, angry with herself for doing it, but somehow quite unable not to. Perhaps now that most of the passengers had gone ashore, he would seek them out.

She arranged the curl in front of her ear with exactitude and jumped visibly when there was a knock on the door and the Professor strolled in, wished them a good morning, made a few noncommittal remarks about the day's activities, asked his patient a few pertinent questions regarding her health and then looked at his watch, remarked that he must be gone, bade Miss Creed goodbye, whisked round on Jenny with surprising speed to kiss her hard and swiftly on her astonished mouth, and went his way.

Aunt Bess's voice broke the silence, to say surprisingly: 'Of course, he's nearly forty.'

Jenny shook the amazement out of her mind. 'That's not old,' she said before she could stop herself.

Her aunt gave her a thoughtful look. 'Heavens, no—did I say it was? And he of all men. . .'

Jenny was staring unseeingly out of the window, to the quay below. She didn't turn round. 'Oh? Why do you say that?'

'Very fit for his age—not an ounce of spare flesh on him. He could make rings round anyone half his age—has a good brain too. He won't look much different when he's seventy, which is more than I can say for some men I know.' She added sternly, 'Toby is not yet thirty and he has a decided bulge.'

Jenny giggled. 'Yes, he has, hasn't he?' And then with elaborate unconcern: 'I don't suppose we shall see Professor van Draak again.'

As to that, child, you're quite out. He wishes to see me from time to time and suggested that I should go over to Holland, where I can have a check-up at the hospital where he's a consultant. It seems to me to be rather a nice idea—I haven't been to Holland for many years and there isn't anything much for me to do at Dimworth. Margaret is there and provided she exerts herself she should be able to manage. Eduard suggested that she might like to accompany me but I couldn't agree to that. You will come with me of course. . .'

Jenny wasn't sure what prompted her to say at once: 'Oh, I couldn't possibly, Aunt Bess,' although she was sure as she said it that there was nothing she would like better. For a man she didn't much like and who didn't much like her, the Professor loomed with an alarming clarity in her mind. The thought of not seeing him again had been niggling away at the back of her mind in a most unpleasant manner.

'Why not, Janet?'

'Well. . .' She sought for an excuse, and came up with: 'I did want to go back to nursing, you know. I thought I might go to Queen's and see if they would take me back. . .'

'If you're short of money. . .' suggested her aunt surprisingly.

Jenny couldn't remember Aunt Bess ever asking her that before. 'I've more than enough, thank you. Aunt Bess; it's not that—I just want to be independent.' As she uttered the words, the niggle exploded into amazing, solid fact; she had no wish to be independent, it was the last thing she wanted to be. She wanted above all things to be married to the Professor and be completely dependent upon him for the rest of her life. Probably they would quarrel, or rather she would quarrel and he would listen and smile in that annoying way of his, but that wouldn't matter in the least; she would love him however tiresome he was. Only he didn't love her. She frowned heavily. That was cold fact and she would have to think about it.

'Well, I expect another few days wouldn't

matter,' she was surprised to hear that her voice sounded perfectly normal. 'How long do you intend staying in Holland?'

'Oh—ten days, perhaps. Eduard wants to do some tests.' Aunt Bess fiddled with a handful of the gold chains she so loved to wear. 'We might see something of the country while we're there; as long as I'm back at Dimworth before we close the house to visitors for the winter.' She dismissed the subject with a wave of the hand. 'And now go and see if we can hire a car, Jenny. I should like a drive—we are here until tomorrow, aren't we?'

Their drive was a rather different one from her trip with the Professor, but Jenny enjoyed it; it passed the morning hours and she had no time to think. Only in the afternoon, while Aunt Bess was resting, could she lie in the sun and think about Eduard van Draak. She would have cheerfully spent her evening doing the same thing, but there was cabaret and dancing and Aunt Bess, feeling festive, insisted that they should join the captain's party after dinner.

They went ashore at Las Palmas too, but although the scenery was delightful and shopping for presents to take home was a pleasant occupation, Jenny hardly noticed any of it. She joined in the cheerful groups of passengers, and laughed and danced when she was asked, but none of it mattered. She was impatient to get back now; the sooner they arrived at Dimworth, the sooner they would go to Holland.

The weather changed as the ship turned for home and Aunt Bess lay in her deckchair in a sheltered corner while Jenny, feeling lost, spent her time in the swimming pool or walked the decks. Now that the Professor was no longer there, the several young men on board were only too anxious to entertain her, but she treated them all with friendly impartiality and gave them no encouragement at all, and when they became too persistent, retired to Aunt Bess's side with the excuse that she must look after her elderly relative.

She danced in the evenings, of course, charming her partners with her sweet smile and ready replies to their talk, but all the while her head was full of the Professor. He had told her once, quite casually, that he had never wanted to marry; he had told her too that he had fallen in and out of love times without number, which was all very well. He had shown no sign of wanting to fall in love with her let alone take her to wife. Jenny smiled and murmured her way through the days, while she considered the best way to capture his serious attention—and that in the face of his interest in Margaret. He had wanted her to accompany Aunt Bess to Holland, hadn't he? and Aunt Bess had refused. Jenny, considering the matter, wondered what he would do next.

But once the ship had docked at Tilbury she had no leisure for her own thoughts. The business of getting Aunt Bess on to firm ground, as well as her considerable luggage, took all her time and attention, and as they went slowly through Customs and out on to the quay she saw to her vexation that it wasn't Aunt Bess's car waiting for them, but Toby in his Rover Metro.

He greeted them with a complacent smile and a: 'Thought I'd give you a surprise. I had some business to do in town anyway. Let's have the luggage, it can go in the boot. There's plenty of room in the back for you, Miss Creed.'

Jenny attempted to thwart this arrangement by declaring that the front seat would be more comfortable for Aunt Bess, but he took no notice and Aunt Bess, strangely enough, raised no objection; indeed she said with some satisfaction: 'I shall do very well in the back, you two will have plenty to say to each other, anyway.' She looked a little cunning as she spoke, but Jenny didn't see that.

Later, thinking about the drive back, Jenny concluded that it had been Toby who had had a great deal to say, and he said it, repeating himself over and over again, giving her a dozen sound reasons why she should agree to marry him. If only he hadn't been so complacent about it, she remembered wearily, taking it for granted that marrying him was the best thing that could hap-

pen to any girl. He was a nice enough man, but
so dull, and he hadn't contradicted her once when
she had argued with him, and even when she
told him firmly that she didn't love him, he
hadn't believed her. If only it had been the
Professor. . .but she couldn't imagine that gentleman behaving so tamely; he would probably have
stopped the car and told her to get out and walk.
She sighed and went in search of Oliver; she had
promised to read to him before he went to bed.

He was curled up on a window seat with
Florrie's sat beside him, doing nothing, which for
him was unusual, and Jenny said at once: 'My,
you're sitting there like a mouse—are you tired?'

He turned to look at her. 'I'm thinking. Do you
think, Jenny?'

On and off. What about—or is it a secret?'

'Mummy and Aunt Bess have had a row—I
heard them because they were in the sitting room
and I was on the stairs. Mummy's cross because
Aunt Bess won't take her to Holland. She says. . .'
he paused to get it right, 'she has a right to go
because she's going to marry Eduard.' He turned
blue eyes on to his listener. 'Who's he?'

Jenny answered faintly: 'Professor van Draak.
You shouldn't listen to other people talking when
they don't know you're there, Oliver.'

Well, I did call to Mummy, but she didn't hear,
they were talking so loudly.' He climbed down
off the window seat and held out a hand. 'Could

we go into the gazebo while you read to me? I'm truly glad you're back, Jenny.'

She bent to kiss him. 'So am I, my lamb—I missed you.'

'But if you go to Holland you'll go away again,' He was faintly tearful.

'So I shall, but I'll be back very soon. Aunt Bess will only be there for a few days, you know. Besides you must stay here and look after Dimworth with Mummy.'

'Mummy doesn't like it here. She only stayed because Professor van Draak was here too.'

'Oh—did she?' She tried to sound casual. 'Well perhaps he'll come and see her.'

Oliver settled himself beside her in the gazebo, for they had walked as they talked. He said wistfully: 'I should like to go to Holland.' He gave her an engaging smile. 'With you, of course, Jenny.'

'And so you shall one day, when you're older and able to buy the tickets and look after me,' she assured him as she opened *Winnie the Pooh*. 'Shall I start reading?'

'Yes, please. Jenny, why haven't you got anyone to look after you? Would Professor van Draak do—if I were to mention it?'

He would do very nicely. Jenny sighed soundlessly. 'No, dear, I don't think so. Now, where were we?'

She settled back into the Dimworth way of life quickly enough. There was plenty to do, for the weather was still good and there were always plenty of visitors. She took her turn sitting at the table in the hall, selling brochures and postcards, helping with the teas, checking the stocks of tea and sugar and scones, polishing and dusting, keeping an eye on Baxter, who had been looking after the gardens for so long now that he tended to forget that they weren't his. . .

They had been back for the best part of a week when Aunt Bess told her that they would be going to Holland in three days' time. She offered this piece of news while they were all having tea, and Oliver burst into tears, while Margaret went white and said in a bitter voice: 'It won't make any difference—Eduard will come here.'

'What makes you think that he is in love with you?' asked Aunt Bess forthrightly. 'Has he actually said to?'

Margaret made a dramatic gesture. 'Not in front of the child,' she remonstrated.

'Pooh, he's bawling so hard he can't hear a word. And don't be dramatic, Margaret. Eduard has had ample opportunity to state his feelings. Personally I am of the opinion that you have imagined the whole thing.'

Margaret rose to her feet. 'I did not—how can you be so unkind? Just because men like me. . . and he doesn't like Jenny and she doesn't like him. They'll both hate it. . .'

Jenny had remained silent, but now she said in

a colourless little voice: 'You forget that it's a professional visit, Margaret; nothing to do with who likes whom, and if you went; the Professor might be distracted from his work.'

Aunt Bess snorted fiercely, 'Rubbish!' and went on ruthlessly: 'Margaret, you will be good enough to remain here and look after Dimworth while we are away—it will do you good to bestir yourself. Go to Holland when we get back by all means—that is no concern of mine, although the mind boggles at the difficulties you will need to surmount. Do you really believe that Eduard will give up his work to come here and live as your consort—because that's what would be. However, that's your concern, as I've already said.' She glanced at Oliver, sitting, beside Jenny blowing his small nose resolutely on the hanky she had offered him. 'We shall take Oliver with us. I enjoy his company.'

'But. . .' Margaret began furiously, then paused and Jenny knew exactly why. Aunt Bess had money, a great deal of it; she had indicated that when she died she would, provided nothing had occurred to annoy her in the meantime, leave most of it to Oliver. Dimworth was by no means a large estate, but it took a good deal of money to run it, and although there was enough for that purpose, her handsome fortune would be a splendid thing for Oliver when he took over his property, and in the meantime his mother would have charge of it. And Margaret liked money.

'Exactly,' nodded Aunt Bess, looking quite wicked and braced herself to receive the rapturous onslaught of her great-nephew.

They left Dimworth in some style. Miss Creed liked to travel in comfort; the Rover Sterling with Dobbs at the wheel would convey them to Holland, and they would stay a night on the way at the small, exclusive hotel in Mayfair where she had always stayed when visiting London before boarding the Hovercraft to take them across the channel. Oliver, sitting in front with Dobbs, was speechless with delight, and Jenny, beside her aunt on the back seat, felt exactly the same. Fortunately for her Aunt Bess dozed for the greater part of the journey, so that she was able to give full rein to her thoughts. About the Professor, of course; she had at last discovered where he lived. North of den Haag, where he had beds in two hospitals, and not too far from Amsterdam, it seemed, for he held a teaching post at the medical school there. Aunt Bess had been annoyingly vague, though—somewhere close to the sea, she had hazarded, and when Jenny had asked where they were to stay she had been even more vague. 'Oh, Eduard has arranged all that,' Jenny was told.

Jenny frowned and hoped that she had brought the right clothes with her. The jersey dress and jacket would do very well for their necessary trips to the hospital and any sightseeing they might do, and she had packed slacks and tops in case there was a chance to take Oliver to the beach. She had added a couple of pretty evening dresses too; presumably they would be staying in an hotel and as Aunt Bess refused to alter her way of life, no matter where she was, Jenny guessed that it would be the kind of place where one dressed for dinner. She reflected rather unhappily that probably she would see almost nothing of the Professor, which was perhaps a good thing, for the more she saw of him the harder it would be to go on pretending that she didn't like him. On the other hand, she couldn't wait to see him again. . .

Safely across the Dutch frontier, Dobbs increased his pace. They would arrive in time for tea; Jenny calculated that while she looked about her at the flat, tranquil countryside. Aunt Bess was dozing again and Oliver, with the faithful Dobbs to answer his whispered questions was fully occupied. Fortunately Dobbs had been in Holland during the second world war and was ready with his answers. At least one member of the party was having a lovely time thought Jenny, smiling at the small coppery head in front of her. Oliver had been delighted at the prospect of spending hours in Dobbs' company while Jenny and Aunt Bess were at the hospital. For one thing he told him stories about the father he could barely remember, and for another he had an unending supply of toffees. She had no doubt that Oliver would be as well looked after as the Crown Jewels.

The country had become wooded and the road they were now on ran straight between trees. There were occasional glimpses of houses on either side, solid villas half hidden behind trees, and every so often a small neat village. It was hard to believe that den Haag and Amsterdam were neither of them far away. Dobbs was looking for signposts now, and presently he turned off into a country road with dense undergrowth on either side and Oliver turned round to Jenny, his face alight with excitement. 'Dobbs says we're there,' he whispered importantly, and pointed.

She looked obediently in the direction of his finger. She could see no hotel, only an open gateway leading to a drive bordered by a rose hedge, meticulously tended, but round the first corner she had her first glimpse of it; an austere, almost mediaeval place built of small red bricks, with narrow windows, a pepperpot tower at either end of its front and a very grand entrance. Old, thought, Jenny, and not in the least like an hotel— probably the owners had had to sell it in order to pay death duties. It would suit Aunt Bess exactly, though—the Professor had chosen well. She roused her aunt gently, set the toque she always wore—just like Aunt Bess's dear queen—

straight on the elegantly dressed head, and prepared to alight.

Oliver was already standing on the gravel sweep, gazing up at the forbidding walls, his small mouth open, while Dobbs opened the car door ready to assist Miss Creed. It was left for Jenny to collect handbags, scarves and all the small paraphernalia with which Aunt Bess travelled, and then get out herself. She did so from the door furthest from the house, so that for the moment she couldn't see the entrance, hidden by the car's substantial bulk, but she heard the Professor's voice and stood still for a moment, catching her surprised breath. She had been looking forward to seeing him with her whole heart, but this was unexpected and she hadn't expected to feel quite like this when she did. It was like jumping off a high diving board, or finding oneself at the top of a mountain—her breath had been taken from her and her heart had shot up into her throat. She swallowed that organ back to where it belonged, steadied her breathing and walked round the back of the car.

He was standing with Aunt Bess, a hand on Oliver's small shoulder, giving some instructions to Dobbs about the luggage and when he saw Jenny he came to meet her. He showed no sign of pleasure at the sight of her—perhaps he had been expecting Margaret—but his greeting was pleasant if a little cool. 'You had a pleasant journey?' he wanted to know. I expect you would like a cup of tea before you do any thing else. Shall we go in?'

The handsome door opened into a square hall of some size, with an enormous hooded fireplace to one side of it, flanked by massive armchairs. The table in the centre was massive too, with a great bowl of flowers on it. The walls held a great many paintings and a variety of weapons; Jenny eyed them as she looked round for the reception desk. There wasn't one, which seemed strange for an hotel—perhaps they didn't have them in Holland. She asked: 'Our rooms are booked, aren't they? I can't see anyone to ask—it's very quiet. . .'

The Professor smiled with quite odious mockery. 'It had better be—I dislike noise in my home.'

'Your home. . .?' She goggled at him. 'I thought—that is, Aunt Bess said. . .'

He answered her blandly. 'A little forgetful, perhaps.'

Jenny gave him a puzzled look. 'Well, yes— perhaps she is. Did you know that Oliver would be with us?'

'Indeed I did.' He was staring at her rather hard. 'A pity that Margaret was unable to come.'

She looked away, studying a nearby portrait of some bygone van Draak te Solendijk; he might have been the Professor with a ruff and a neat little beard. . . She said soberly: 'I'm sorry about that, truly I am.' She frowned in thought. 'You know, once Aunt Bess is dealt with there's no reason why I shouldn't go back to Dimworth and she could come here. . .'

'My dear Jenny, I had no idea that you had such a kind heart—as far as I'm concerned, that is. I'm sure it does you credit.'

She glanced to where Aunt Bess and Oliver were absorbed in a vast painting of some sea battle or other. 'You have no need to be nasty,' she observed coldly, 'just because it's me here instead of Margaret. I didn't want to come,' she added with a complete lack of truth.

'I? Nasty? My dear girl, you are mistaken—I merely protect myself. Your poet Aaron Hill wrote something a long time ago—let me see— "Tender-handed stroke a nettle and it stings you for your pains; grasp it like a man of mettle and it soft as silk remains." Er—I daresay you can be as soft as silk, Jenny—you certainly sting.'

'What a perfectly beastly. . .' She was interrupted by Aunt Bess, her compelling voice uplifted.

'Some good paintings here,' she observed, 'comparable to those at Dimworth—probably better,' she conceded graciously.

The Professor was too well mannered to agree. He made a deprecating sound and led the lady towards the double doors to one side of the hall. They were opened from the inside by a short, stout man with a solemn face, whom the Professor addressed as Hans. He bowed with great dignity to the ladies and endeared himself greatly to Jenny by winking at Oliver, who winked back, delighted.

Tea was all that Aunt Bess could have wished for; thin cucumber sandwiches, a cake as light as air, little sugary biscuits, and tea poured from a silver tea-pot. And their surroundings matched the meal in elegance—a lovely room, long and narrow, furnished with what Jenny described to herself as Dimworth furniture. Only the curtains were a great deal more elaborate; thick brocaded velvet in a rich crimson, swathed and looped and fringed. She liked them, just as she liked the great chairs and dainty little tables and the enormous glass-fronted cabinet between the high, narrow windows.

'Is it open to the public?' asked Oliver.

The Professor handed cake to Aunt Bess. 'No, I'm afraid not. You see, Oliver, I should have to be at home a good deal if I were to do that, and I'm not—I'm at the hospital or my consulting rooms for a long time each day.'

Very nicely put, decided Jenny; probably the idea of helping out the revenue by charging so much a head to look round his home had never entered the Professor's head. Probably he was rich—well, he would have to be to live in such a house; large and difficult to heat, she suspected, and certainly needing a number of people to look after it. She longed to see more of it, and the wish was granted when he asked.

'Would you like to see your rooms? Miss Creed, I hope you will feel well enough to come to the hospital in den Haag tomorrow. There are several tests I should like to do—they won't take long, and it would be a good idea to get them over and done with.'

'Whatever you say, Eduard.' Aunt Bess sounded gracious and almost meek.

They went upstairs then, under the guidance of a small round woman, no longer young but very bustling in manner, with a cheerful face and pepper-and-salt hair severely dressed—Hans' wife, Hennie, the Professor had told them as she smiled a welcome, took Oliver by the hand and led them up the gracefully curved staircase to the floor above.

Their rooms were at the side of the house, close together, with Jenny's in the middle, separated from her aunt by a bathroom, and from Oliver by a communicating door. Hennie indicated that she would unpack for Miss Creed, and fussed her gently and not unwillingly into a chair, which left Jenny free to inspect her own room while Oliver ran backwards and forwards, inviting her urgently to look at this and that and the other thing in his own room. She smiled and nodded and said a little absently: 'Yes, in a moment, dear,' and went on with her tour of inspection. The room was furnished in a later period than the house had been built—Hepplewhite, with the bed, canopied with muslin, of satinwood, as was the dressing table and mirror upon it and the tallboy against one wall. The chairs were made for comfort, upholstered in pale pink striped silk, matching the curtains. The lamps were a rosy pink too and there were a variety of small silver and china ornaments which exactly suited the pale pastel portraits on the panelled walls. 'Very nice,' said Jenny out loud, and kicked off a shoe to feel the thickness of the moss green carpet.

Oliver returned hopefully to say: 'Isn't it super—do you think all the other rooms are like this one? It's a bit like Dimworth.'

'Yes, my lamb, though I think it's a good deal older than Dimworth.'

'Wait until I tell Mummy! Is he very rich?'

'And who is *he*?' asked Jenny reprovingly. 'If you mean Professor van Draak, I have no idea, but I should suppose he might be. It's no business of ours darling.' She was admiring a delicate porcelain figure she had picked up from a little work-table, and Oliver had gone to look out of the mullioned window.

'You don't sound as though you want to know Jenny. Mummy does—she said it mattered. Does it matter?'

She put the figure back carefully and gave him

her full attention. 'Not one little bit, Oliver.'

And it didn't; she would settle most willingly for a completely penniless Professor, and if necessary live in one of those dreadful little modern houses like boxes, wearing last year's clothes and cooking cheap wholesome meals for him and the happy brood of children they would undoubtedly have. She was so lost in her daydream that she only just heard the little boy say in a small voice: 'Mummy wants to marry the Professor.'

Put into words, even a child's words, it sounded very final, but Jenny made a great effort. 'Well, dear, your mummy is a very pretty lady, you know, and although she loved your daddy very much, she feels lonely.'

'So do I. Professor van Draak wouldn't be happy. . .'

She went and knelt beside him and put her arms round his small shoulders. 'Why not, love?'

'Not at Dimworth—he's a surgeon.' His voice implied that she had asked a silly question, but Jenny was spared having to answer this awkward but wise remark by the loud barking of a dog, a distraction which sent Oliver to the window again, his worries forgotten. 'Oh, look—Jenny, it's two dogs and a cat, and the Professor's with them. May I go down?'

She went to look as she had been bidden. The grounds stretched away below them, turf with herbaceous borders leading to more open ground, well shrubbed and with trees in the distance as well as the gleam of water. The Professor was strolling across the grass, a great Dane treading beside him while a dog of extremely mixed parentage gavotted round them, while bringing up the rear was a very ordinary tabby cat.

'Very well, dear, but ask the Professor if you may go with him, don't just attach yourself to him.'

'He won't mind,' declared Oliver, making for the door. 'He likes boys, he said so, he's been a boy himself.'

Jenny turned her back on the window and unpacked before going to see how her aunt fared. 'I shall change for dinner,' declared that lady. 'You will go and tell Eduard so, Jenny, and come back in half an hour to help me with my hair before you dress.'

Jenny eyed her aunt doubtfully. 'Perhaps the Professor doesn't bother to change when he's home,' she offered, to be met with a positive: 'He has guests and will behave accordingly, Janet.'

She went slowly downstairs and out of the house door. The Professor, Oliver and the animals were already some distance away, making for the water—presumably a pond. Jenny reached them as they came to a halt at its edge to watch the ducks upon it, and they all turned round to look at her.

'Everything all right?' he wanted to know, and

she had the feeling that he hadn't wanted her there. It made her say with a touch of haughtiness: 'Perfectly, thank you. Aunt Bess asked me to let you know that she intends dressing for dinner.'

He raised his eyebrows. 'How thoughtful of her—but hardly necessary.'

Jenny went pink. 'No—well, she didn't mean it like that. It's just that she's a little set in her ways.'

She waited uncertainly while he dug a hand into a pocket and handed Oliver a crust of bread. 'There you are, boy, and don't fall in.'

Oliver lifted adoring eyes to the big man's face. 'You do think of everything, don't you?' He started towards the reeds where the ducks were and then came back. 'Do I have to have my supper with you?'

His host smiled. 'No, I think not. Hennie will give you your supper when he gets back to the house and see you safely to bed. She's very kind.'

'Have you any more servants?' Oliver wanted to know, and Jenny said: 'Hush, my lamb, that's rude!'

But the Professor answered, just as though she hadn't said anything: 'Oh, yes, several, but Hennie is my old friend as well as my housekeeper and she will look after you especially well.'

Oliver nodded and wandered off happily, leaving Jenny to apologise for his lack of manners. 'But he's only six,' she explained.

Her companion had stooped to pick up the cat. 'I wasn't aware that I had complained about the boy,' he observed blandly. 'I expect you have things to do—I'll bring him back to the house presently.'

She wanted very much to burst into tears; he was rude and arrogant and quite unfeeling, and she hated him! No, hate was too good a word, she loathed him. She said in an icy voice: 'You don't have to take it out on me just because I'm here and Margaret isn't. I didn't ask to come, and now I wish I hadn't. . .'

She flounced off, using considerable self-control in not looking back, and having gained her room, spent a few minutes thinking up all the awful things she would like to happen to him. Considerably cheered by this exercise, she made her way to Aunt Bess's room, where she performed all the small tasks demanded of her and then went back to her own room once more, to dress herself carelessly in the first thing that came to hand, sweep her glowing hair into a severe knot, slap powder on to her pretty nose and put on the wrong lipstick. 'Who cares?' she asked her reflection ferociously, and went next door to see if Oliver was in bed.

He wasn't exactly in bed, but at least he was pottering happily around his room with Hennie in loving attendance. Jenny wrung a promise from him that he would be in bed in exactly ten minutes and went downstairs to join the others. She found them in the drawing room, chatting amiably, and because she was well brought up, she chatted too, seething beneath the bodice of her flowered silk dress. She ate her dinner too with every appearance of enjoyment, only her eyes flashed temper at her host when he addressed her, even though she schooled her tongue to utter platitudes by way of answer.

They sat a long while over their meal, round a mahogany table decked with silver and crystal and spotless white linen. The room was square and of a good size, and Jenny, peeping round her whenever she had the opportunity, loved its rich amber curtains and needlework carpet and the dark panelling of the walls. The Professor lived in comfort—not that he deserved it. She scowled at the idea and looked up find his eyes upon her. His smile, knowing and mocking, made her scowl even fiercer.

It was when they had gone to the drawing room and had taken their coffee in a leisurely fashion, that the Professor had suggested to his patient that perhaps an early night might be of benefit to her, doing it in such a way that she was unaware that he had made the suggestion in the first place, only remarking that she considered it high time that they were all in bed as she rose to her feet. He got up too, walking unhurriedly to the door with her, crossing the hall, still talking casually before bidding her goodnight at the foot of the staircase. Jenny behind them, made to go upstairs too, but he caught her firmly as she passed him so that she was forced to stand still.

'I will settle the details about your visit to the hospital with Jenny, Miss Creed,' he suggested smoothly. 'I'm sure you won't wish to be bothered with them.'

'Very considerate,' agreed Aunt Bess, turning to look at them from halfway up the staircase. 'And don't keep Eduard up unnecessarily, Jenny; he has had a busy day. I'm sure.' She went on her stately way and turned once more to remark: 'A delicious dinner, Eduard. Goodnight.'

Her majestic back disappeared from sight and the Professor's hold slackened. 'We can't talk here, shall we go back to the drawing room?'

Jenny went with him, saying nothing at all. If he wanted to give her some instructions, let him do so she couldn't stop him. But when they were once more sitting facing each her he asked: 'What exactly did you mean about Margaret?'

'What I said. And if that's all you want to talk about, I think I will go to bed.'

'Carved from an ice block,' he mused, 'with your "Yes, Professor, no, Professor" as meek as you like, and your eyes killing me. Tell me, Jenny, do you really dislike me so much? Oh, I tease you deliberately just to see you get angry, but is that sufficient reason for you to treat me as though I had the plague?'

He crossed to her chair and pulled her to her feet, holding her hands fast in his, and turned her round on that the lamplight shone on to her face. 'Well—Do you dislike me?'

She must have been made to have supposed that she loathed him—hated him, even disliked him—how could that be possible when she loved him so much? He was the only man she would ever want to marry, she knew that for certain, and if he married Margaret her heart would break, but he mustn't be allowed to even guess at that. She said stonily: 'No, I don't like you, Professor van Draak,' because there was nothing else she could have said. And it couldn't matter to him in the least what she thought of him if he were in love with Margaret. Supposing she said 'I love you very much', what would he do? she wondered miserably. Despite his mocking smile and his nasty remarks he was a kind man, she was sure of that, and he would feel badly if she let him see that she had a *tendresse* for him.

He let her hands go and smiled a little. 'One of the nastiest stings the nettle has given me so far,' he declared lightly, 'but it's best to clear the air, isn't it?' He moved a little away and pulled the great dane's ears gently and went on pleasantly: 'Will you come with your aunt tomorrow? It may make things easier for her.

There isn't a great deal to do—a sample of blood and I should like to do a scan...one or two tests...they should take two or three hours, no more. Hans will drive you there and bring you back, that will leave Dobbs free to stay with Oliver. I was going to suggest that you both came with me in the morning, but I think now that it would be better if Hans takes you. I should like Miss Creed to rest when she comes back here; there will be several more tests and I don't want her to get tired. Three days should suffice, for I don't intend to overtax her strength.'

He smiled down at her, so kindly that Jenny only just prevented herself from putting out a hand to catch his sleeve and tell him what her true feelings were. But that would never do; she agreed politely promised to have her aunt ready at the required hour and wished him goodnight. He didn't walk with her to the door and she didn't look back as she went out of the room.

CHAPTER SEVEN

JENNY found the next three days difficult even though they were interesting. The Professor treated her with the courtesy of a good host, but as he confined his conversations with her to her aunt's condition, suggestions as to times of appointments and similar dull topics; even if she had wanted to retract every word she had said on that first evening, it would have been impossible to get through the invisible but none the less solid barrier he had erected between them. After all, before, despite their disagreements, there had been a certain camaraderie between them, now there was nothing at all.

But if she was unhappy, Oliver was in the seventh heaven; with Dobbs as an ever-watchful companion, he had gone sightseeing; to the Maduradam at den Haag, to a number of castles in the vicinity and to the coast to see the sea and play on the sands. And when he wasn't at one or other of these places, he was pottering in a small rowboat on the pond, learning to use the oars under Hans' guidance, or eating the satisfying meals Hennie prepared for him. Life for him, at least, was bliss.

Aunt Bess seemed content enough too. True, her days were largely taken up with visits to the hospital and the rather wearisome hours there, and there were occasional visits to the Professor's consulting rooms too, but as these were organised with an eye to her comfort and convenience, she bore them with an equanimity which Jenny found nothing short of astonishing.

On their first visit to the hospital, driven there by Hans very shortly after breakfast, they had been met in the entrance hall by an elderly Sister whose English, although heavily accented, was more than adequate. She had whisked them away to the Surgical Floor and installed them in a waiting room, and Aunt Bess had barely had the time to complain at being kept waiting before a nurse came to usher them into the Professor's own sanctum.

It was much like any other consulting room. Jenny decided that if it hadn't been for some books on the shelves with ponderous-looking Dutch titles, it might have been in England, and indeed, when she looked more closely, there were a great many books with English titles, too, as well as French and German.

The Professor had risen from behind his desk to greet them and it was at once obvious that was no longer Eduard but Professor van Draak, about to examine his patient. Aunt Bess, ever one to speak her mind, had remarked upon this

immediately with a: 'Ah—professional treatment, is it? I must remember not to call you
Eduard. Jenny, take my jacket, I can't think why
I brought it with me in the first place. Now, what
am I to do first?'

The examination had progressed satisfactorily;
from time to time Aunt Bess had demurred about
something or other, but only because she felt
bound to do so, and she was easily overborne by
the Professor, suavely having his own way. Jenny,
sitting silently close by, getting up and doing what
she was required to do in her usual sensible
fashion, couldn't help but admire the ease with
which he managed his patient. At the same time
she deplored the fact that he took absolutely no
notice of herself. But that was her own fault.

Hans took them back to Kasteel te Solendijk
afterwards, to a late lunch without the Professor,
before Jenny settled her aunt for a nap. Having
done which she felt free to do whatever she liked
until teatime.

On that first afternoon she had toured the house
with Hennie, and come to the conclusion that
although it was vastly different from Dimworth,
it was just as lovely, and certainly its contents
were a good deal older, as was the house itself.
She had remarked this at dinner that evening and
the Professor had thanked her gravely without
offering any further comment. This had the effect
of making her feel peevish, so that she was glad

when her aunt decided to go to bed very shortly after they had had their coffee and she was able to make her own excuses. Of course, if their host had even so much as hinted that he would enjoy her society for the evening, she would have changed her mind on the instant, but he did no such thing, only wished her a formal goodnight, which had the unhappy effect of rendering her sleepless.

The next day and the day after that were very much the same; Jenny, not sleeping well, presented a tired, pale face at breakfast, and it was perhaps as well that their host had already left in the morning before she and Oliver got downstairs, and if he did notice her quietness, he didn't remark upon it, although he was pleasant enough in a remote way and very considerate of her comfort as well as that of her aunt. And on the third morning, while she waited for Aunt Bess in the X-ray department, he sought her out to tell her that if she wished, one of the Sisters would take her round the hospital.

It was an enjoyable hour. Her guide had been a girl of her own age whose English, although limited, was enthusiastic. She was the Children's Ward Sister and they went there first, and Jenny, very impressed with the bright, cheerful place, peered and poked and asked endless questions before going to the Surgical Block; they spent so much time there that they had had to skimp the

Medical side in order to see the Theatre Wing.
Here Jenny was on home ground, and the two of
them became immersed in a discussion on the
best equipment for the recovery room and how
it should be run, the number of nurses necessary
to deal with it all, and they had their heads
together over the newest thing in pumps for heart
surgery when a student nurse came to tell them
that the Professor was waiting for them.

They found him at the entrance, looking
impatient, and Jenny made haste to apologise,
still so full of her tour that she forgot to be distant
with him. 'I got carried away,' she explained.
'There was such a lot to see in the Theatre Block.'

'I'm glad you found it interesting,' he told her
repressively, and then turned to say something in
a quite different tone of voice to her guide, who
smiled and nodded and looked pleased with
herself before shaking Jenny's hand and
hurrying away.

'Your aunt refused to wait for you,' said the
Professor crossly. 'You will have to come with
me—I'll drop you off on my way.'

'Where to?' asked Jenny, and regretted her
words when he replied, still cross:

'Since you are curious enough to ask—
Amsterdam.'

He walked towards the door and a porter hurried after them to open it, and she was ushered
out to the forecourt where the Panther de Ville

was parked. They didn't speak at all until he drew up before his own front door, and when Jenny said politely: 'Thank you very much, Professor,' all she got was a curt: 'Well, don't expect me to say that it was a pleasure,' a remark which cast her into the depths for the remainder of that day.

There were to be no more tests for Aunt Bess, only a few days waiting for the results, so that she declared that she would enjoy a little peace and quiet in the gardens, recruiting her strength, and Jenny, egged on by Oliver, suggested that the pair of them might go to Amsterdam and have a look round. 'Oliver's dying to go, and so am I,' she declared. 'If Dobbs would drive us there, we could come back by train and telephone when we get to the station and he can pick us up there.'

The Professor wasn't there to cast a damper on her suggestion, and Aunt Bess could see no harm in it. Jenny was warned to take good care of Oliver, make sure that she had sufficient money with her and took care what they ate, and allowed to make her plans.

It seemed prudent to make them while the Professor was still absent, so that when the subject was broached at dinner that evening, there was really nothing much he could do about it, although she could see that he didn't approve. She sat, a delightful picture in the silvery crêpe dress she had put on with the mistaken idea that it made her look inconspicuous, her eyes on her plate, so that the lashes curled on her cheeks, trying not to look pleased because he was, for once, not to have his own way.

She could see no reason at all why she and Oliver shouldn't go to Amsterdam; Dobbs could drop them off in the heart of the city and from there they could take a canal boat and tour the waterways before having a good look at the shops. Left to herself she would have visited as many museums as she could have crowded into the time available, but one could hardly expect a lively six-year-old boy to do that—besides, he wanted to buy his mother a present. They would have lunch too, somewhere well-known; Jenny had a guide book and had ticked off the most likely restaurants.

She mentioned all this reluctantly to her host, but only because she was unable to do anything else in the face of his direct questions. His final grunt of disapproval made her all the more determined to go. It was ridiculous that he should consider her incapable of spending a day out without coming to grief.

And it was infuriating to watch his nasty little smile. She could imagine him saying 'I told you so' if by some remote chance their day should go awry. Spurred on by the smile, she remarked defiantly: 'It will be a day to remember,' and added for good measure: 'I don't suppose you enjoy that sort of thing any more.'

He had looked at her then with a sudden cold anger which caught the breath in her throat, aware that she had been rude and unkind too. She wanted to get up and run to him and beg his forgiveness and tell him that she hadn't meant a word of it. Who was it who had said that one always wanted to hurt the one one loved? How very true! She had actually made a movement to rise when Aunt Bess, silent too long, began a rambling dissertation on the intricacies of family history, which allowed of neither of her listeners speaking until she had finished, and by then it was too late. All the same, Jenny tried again when they left the table, asking diffidently if he had a few minutes to spare her as she had something she wished to say to him, to be instantly snubbed with a chilly civility which froze her bones.

'Unfortunately I have several important telephone calls to make,' he told her with a smile which didn't reach his eyes. 'Tomorrow, perhaps?'

But of course he had left the house by the time she and Oliver got downstairs; moreover, Hans told her that the master of the house expected to be late home that evening and trusted that his guests would excuse him.

'So that's that,' sighed Jenny, and because it was Oliver's day, applied herself to the excitements lying head of them.

They left soon after breakfast, having bidden

Aunt Bess goodbye and made sure that she had
all she wanted before getting into the car with
Dobbs at the wheel. Jenny, on the back seat by
herself, studied her map of Amsterdam once more
and then at back to view the countryside. It was
a fine day with a blue sky and a brisk wind and
little chance of rain, which was a good thing for
to please Oliver she had put on a pale blue jersey
dress he particularly liked. If it rained it would
be tiresome, but there would be shelter enough
in the city and Hans had assured her that there
were plenty of trains running when they wanted
to return.

Dobbs didn't like leaving them when they
reached the square in front of the main station;
he spent quite five minutes trying to persuade
them to get back into the car while he drove them
on a personally conducted tour of the city, until
Jenny said gently: 'Look, Dobbs, it isn't that we
wouldn't like to come with you, it's just that we
want to escape—just an hour or two. . .'

He understood her well enough and grinned in
sympathy as he said goodbye, leaving them to
join the queue for a canal boat.

The trip was exciting because they were in
foreign city and everything looked different,
especially from the canals: the funny little gabled
houses with their windows overlooking the water,
the enormous mansions with their high windows
and great doors, the narrow bridges and the

people walking or cycling along the streets along-
side them, even a street organ belting out some
jolly tune which exactly suited their mood. As
they stepped out of the boat, Oliver wheedled:
'Let's do it again, Jenny—please! I want to look
at it all—it was so quick. . .look, there's another
boat just going to leave!'

Jenny laughed at him. 'All right, my lamb, but
I'll have to race to get the tickets. Wait here.'

There were quite a lot of people round the
ticket booths even though the tourist season was
almost over now. Foreigners like herself, she
thought resignedly, waiting her turn. It was a
minute or two before she had her new tickets and
made her way back to where she had left Oliver.
He wasn't there; she looked round carefully, for
he couldn't be far away. But he was; she heard
his shrill voice calling her name gleefully and
turned round once more to see the boat gliding
away at a great rate with him waving from a seat
in the middle. He was perfectly happy, indeed
she could see that he was laughing. She just had
time to memorise the number of the boat before
it disappeared under the first bridge; there was
nothing to do for it but to remain where she was
until it returned, almost an hour away.

She found a stone wall to sit on and fell to
pondering what she should do. Must Oliver be
punished by being taken straight back to the
Professor's house? But probably he hadn't done

it deliberately, only become impatient and gone on board in his eagerness not to miss a further treat.

And if he had done it deliberately, wasn't it the kind of thing all little boys did at some time or other? Margaret didn't allow him much freedom and he led a dull life. . . Jenny sensibly decided to wait and see what he had to say for himself when he got back, and waited patiently for the hour to pass while a dozen frightening possibilities chased themselves round and round inside her head.

The waiting time seemed long; when she saw the boat at last she made herself walk unhurriedly to the spot where it would berth, prepared to use more patience, for the boat was very full. But she knew real panic when the last passenger disembarked and there was no Oliver. There were already people boarding the craft for the next trip and she wormed her way through them, oblivious of the annoyed glances around her, and found the guide.

'A little boy,' she said breathlessly, 'six years with coppery-red-hair. He got on while I was getting the tickets. He hasn't come back.'

The guide was a tall girl with a cheerful face, 'I saw him,' she spoke in excellent English, 'he sat over there.' She pointed to a seat halfway along the gang way. 'He was talking to the people with him—I thought he belonged to them.' She paused. 'Not?' she wanted to know.

'Not,' said Jenny soberly. 'Did he get off, with them? I didn't know these boats stopped.'

The guide nodded. 'I am sure that he did. We are not supposed to stop, but sometimes if it is something very special, and these people were Dutch and had a reason—the lady felt sick.'

Jenny's mouth had gone dry, but she said steadily: 'Please will you tell me where that was? I must find him—he'll be lost. . .'

'Just past the Leidesstraat; we go under a bridge there and there is another canal crossing the Heerengracht at that point. There is a small landing stage there—we stopped for only a minute.'

'I don't even know where it is,' said Jenny wildly, and then, common sense coming to her aid: 'Thank you very much, you've been very kind—I'll get a taxi.'

The intending passengers were milling all round her now, annoyed at being delayed. It took her a few minutes to get off the boat, for as fast as she made for the exit, she was pushed back by a fresh wave of incoming people. Once on the quay she made herself stand still and think sensibly. Oliver had some money with him—not much, though, and although he was an adventurous little boy she didn't think that he would do anything foolish. He might even think of taking a taxi back to the boat stage. She went back to the ticket booth and found someone there who understood English. 'If a small boy with red hair comes here, will you please ask him to wait? That I'll be back very soon. I'm going to look for him.' She repeated the words for a second time, not quite sure that her listener understood, and finally turned away.

The Professor was so close behind her that she tumbled into him and had to catch his sleeve to avoid falling. Her spontaneous, 'Eduard—oh, thank heaven you're here!' was uttered before she remembered that they weren't on speaking terms any more, it seemed quite right and natural that he should be there when she wanted him, so she gave him a shaky smile, unaware that her face was quite white and that she looked scared out of her wits. 'I've lost Oliver—he got on the boat while I was getting the tickets. . .' The whole story tumbled out in a cascade of words, half of which didn't make sense.

The Professor removed her hands from his coat sleeve. 'So he has been gone for just over an hour.' His eyes, very cold and blue, stared down into hers. 'He could be anywhere. We will go to the landing stage you speak of and find out if anyone saw him leave the boat and which direction he took. If we draw a blank, we will go to the police.'

He walked her across the street to a taxi rank and told her to get into the cab. When he was seated beside her, he asked: 'How much money had he with him?'

'About twenty gulden—he was going to buy his mother a present.' Jenny spoke in a carefully controlled voice, her hands gripping each other tightly on her lap, while a procession of all the frightful things which could happen to a small lost boy wove its way through her brain.

At the landing stage she made herself stand quietly while the Professor made some enquiries and at the third attempt had success.

An old man, sitting on a stool, smoking and watching the world go by. He remembered Oliver quite clearly; the boy had stood for a few moments talking to a man and woman who had apparently been pointing out the way to him, for he had waved quite cheerfully to them and gone off down the *steeg* between the general stores and the tobacconists—and furthermore, in answer to the Professor's persistent questions, the boy had seemed perfectly happy—certainly not frightened. That was the extent of his memory. The Professor rewarded him suitably and rejoined Jenny.

She said at once: 'You've got news, haven't you? Is he all right? Where is he?' Her mouth, despite her best efforts, shook a little. 'I'm very sorry. . .'

'A little late in the day for that,' remarked her companion severely. 'Of all the silly things to do. . .however, that can wait. He went down this *steeg*, I imagine, on his way to the shops, for they can be reached from here, provided one knows the way I suggest that we walk down it now, searching every passage leading off it. You take that side, I will take this, and we will meet at the end. He may have fallen down or lost his way—the *steegs* all look alike—he may even be asleep in some corner, so look well. Can you whistle?'

Jenny understood him at once. 'Yes.'

'That is at least something to be thankful for,' he commented drily. 'One long and two short if you find him—and stay with him, for pity's sake.'

She had no idea of doing anything else, but she supposed she deserved his scorn and set off meekly beside him, to turn into the first narrow passage after a few yards. She went to its end—a blank wall, part of a factory, she supposed, and the tiny, derelict houses on either side showed no sign of life either. She retraced her footsteps and encountered the Professor returning from a similar search on his side, and parted from him almost immediately to turn into the next alley, with high walls on either side this time and ending in a shed neatly piled with bits and pieces of old cars. She searched every inch of it before going back, this time to see her companion's large back disappearing down a similar passage on his side. The next *steeg* wound itself between small houses at first and then blank walls again. Jenny had

gone halfway down its length when she saw
Oliver ahead of her, coming in her direction. He
had a boy on either side of him, both coloured
and in their early teens, each holding a hand.
Jenny began to run, tearing over the cobbles at a
great rate, calling his name in little gusty breaths
while all the while she was wondering what he
was doing there and who were the boys. Was he
being kidnapped? He was calling to her now,
but she didn't stop to listen—supposing the boys
turned and ran off with him before she could
reach them? She didn't see the banana skin on
the ground; she skidded along the cobbles and
fell, banging her head, aware at the last split
second that she had knocked herself out.

When she opened her eyes, it was to encounter
the Professor's blazing down at her, so that she
closed them again at once, unwilling to face such
fury. But she heard him say furiously: 'Why the
hell didn't you whistle?' and before she could
answer that: 'No don't talk. Oliver is here safe—
these two boys were showing him the way back.
His sense of adventure got the better of him, I
fancy. You will stay exactly as you are while I
get a taxi.'

Which remark naturally made her want to sit
up immediately. 'I'm perfectly all right,' she said
in a voice which wasn't quite steady.

'I know that,' he sounded annoyingly matter-
of-fact about it, 'but you cut your head a little

and knocked yourself out. You should pay more attention to where you are going.'

It was really the last straw—to be hauled over the coals like this when she had been doing her utmost. . .'Oh, stop pointing out my faults!' she cried furiously. 'That's all you do. . .I'm sick and tired. . .'

He said something she couldn't understand because it was in his own language and she didn't bother to open her eyes because her head ached. She felt his arm slide from her shoulders and instead Oliver's small hand wormed its way into hers. His voice, a little worried, whispered in her ear: 'Jenny, I didn't mean to frighten you, truly I didn't—I thought I'd look for a present for Mummy and then we would have more time for lunch. I was going to come back, but I got lost. Those boys were super—the Professor gave them some money. He's gone to get a taxi.'

She opened her eyes then and smiled at the small, earnest face peering down at her. 'Yes, my lamb.'

'You're not cross? He wasn't.'

She gave the Professor a good mark for that; he must understand children. 'No, I'm not cross—not a bit. Only you frightened me a little, Oliver—you see, you knew where you'd gone, but I didn't. Next time just let me know before you go, then I shan't worry. But it's really a much better idea to know your way around before you go off on your own—I'm sure the Professor would agree with that.'

She closed her eyes again and then opened them quickly because the taxi had arrived and she felt a fool, propped up against the wall, looking, she felt sure, like nothing on earth. And indeed, looking down at herself, she was a sight; the dress was a ruin for a start, for she had caught her heel in it as she fell, and the bodice was covered with small flecks of blood. Worse, her hair had come loose and was hanging round her shoulders in a very tatty fashion.

The Professor bent to lift her from the street and she protested fiercely—a waste of time and breath, for he didn't even bother to answer her, just settled her in the taxi, lifted Oliver into the seat by the driver, and then got in beside her.

'We can't go home,' she muttered.

'Not at once. You are going to have that head attended to and then we will have lunch—a meal will do you good. We can go home later.'

She would have argued about that, but her head was beginning to ache again. All the same, she asked: 'How did you know where we were?'

'Dobbs had already told me where you intended to go, and if you remember, you mentioned it yourself during dinner yesterday evening. And now stop talking and give that headache a chance.'

Jenny hadn't really bothered to think where

she was being taken. It was only as the taxi drew up before a quite obvious hospital entrance that she exclaimed: 'Oh, there's no need for me to go here!'

'Be quiet,' said the Professor, and lifted her out, keeping an arm round her while he paid the driver. 'Go the other side of Jenny,' he told Oliver, 'and take her hand.'

For such a small cut she felt that a great deal of fuss was being made; perhaps because the Professor was known; he would be a consultant there, of course, which accounted for the immediate response to his wishes. She was provided with tea, sat comfortably in a chair and had her head examined carefully under his watchful eyes before the wound was cleaned, covered, and her hair combed and tied back neatly. She felt quite herself by now and was able to exchange a few words with the Sister and nurse who had helped her, given her an ATS injection and assured her that she had nothing to worry about before handing her back to the Professor with a tender care which he, however, didn't reflect. His casual: 'OK?' was presumably all that he felt it necessary to say before walking her out to the forecourt. True, his arm was under hers, but he would have done that for anyone who had just knocked themselves out. . .

The Panther de Ville was there; he must have fetched it from somewhere—the hospital itself perhaps? That made sense. What didn't make sense was the direction they took, for in a very few minutes they were driving down the Singel, the innermost semi-circular canal of the four principal ones which ringed the city, and Jenny wasn't so silly that she didn't know that travelling into the city's heart wouldn't get them on the road to den Haag. He had said something about a meal; perhaps he had a favourite restaurant. She felt hungry then, although she hoped that it wouldn't be too noisy, thoughts which led naturally enough to remembering the state of her dress. She couldn't possibly be seen in it—only a man, she thought crossly, would ignore such an important point.

Only the Professor hadn't ignored it; he turned into a narrow street lined with elegant houses and small shops and stopped outside one of them. He got out, saw Oliver safely on to the pavement and then opened the car door again. 'Feel up to buying a dress?' he asked casually. 'You can't go round in that thing.'

She stiffened; 'that thing' had cost her a pretty penny not so long ago, although she had to admit that now it wasn't fit to be seen. She allowed herself to be escorted into the shop—and a very elegant shop too—and wondered how he knew of it in the first place. The saleswoman knew him too; she smiled and chattered for a few moments and then broke into very fair English.

'I have just the dress for you, miss—not such a charming blue, but elegant.' She beamed widely. 'Miss has a charming figure.' A remark which drew no response from any of them as Jenny was led away to the fitting room.

The dress was pretty, duck egg blue jersey, with wide sleeves and an open neck and with a silk blouse of a paler shade to wear beneath it. It was a perfect fit too, but when Jenny asked its price the saleswoman seemed suddenly bereft of all knowledge of English so that Jenny was forced to ask the Professor's help. But before he answered her request, he took a long look, said: 'I like it, don't you, Oliver?' and then went on: 'I'll settle for it now, you can pay me later.'

Which he proceeded to do without waiting for her reply. She thanked him as they got back into the car, but he only nodded carelessly and said: 'Now for lunch.'

She wondered where they were going next. He had reversed the car smartly and was back in the Singel, only to turn away from it again down a quiet, treelined street, bordered by tall, narrow houses, each with double steps leading to an imposing door. There was a canal running down the centre of the street and the willow trees beside it rustled gently in the wind. It was a charming backwater, left over from the Golden Age, and Jenny exclaimed: 'Oh, how delightfully peaceful!' and then looked enquiringly at the Professor when he stopped before one of the houses.

'My mother and father live here,' he observed as he got out of the car, helped her out and then gave Oliver a hand. 'They will be delighted to invite you for lunch.'

Jenny uttered a surprised 'Oh,' and then racked her brain for something else to say—something graceful and polite as befitted the occasion. She could think of nothing suitable, so contented herself with: 'Well, I am surprised.'

'Why?'

They were crossing the brick pavement with Oliver prancing along beside them. 'Well, I didn't suppose—that is, you never mentioned your family. . .'

'There are quite a few things I haven't mentioned.' He smiled his mocking smile and Jenny frowned and looked away. 'I had no idea that you were interested. Should I feel flattered?'

'I'm quite sure that you get all the flattery you could wish for,' she told him crossly as he banged the brass knocker on a door strong enough to withstand a siege.

An elderly woman, very tall and thin and dressed in black, admitted them. She greeted the Professor warmly, smiled at Jenny and Oliver and waved a hand towards one of the doors in the narrow panelled hall. Jenny found herself borne along, the Professor's large, cool hand under her elbow, Oliver hanging on to her other hand. She

supposed it was the bang she had had on her head
which made the morning's happenings seem so
unreal. It was like being in a dream where one
had no power to do what one wished; the
Professor had taken charge without so much as
a by-your-leave—not that she would have been
capable of doing much about anything. She felt
sick just remembering her fright when she had
discovered that Oliver had gone, and something
of her feelings must have shown on her face, for
her companion asked unexpectedly: 'Do you feel
all right? Would you prefer to lie down?'

'No—thank you.' She gave him a grave look.
'Aren't you angry with me?'

His face was grave too. 'Yes, but probably not
for the same reasons—and this is hardly the time
or the place, is it?'

He opened the door and stood aside to let her
pass him. The room was long and lofty and rather
dim, with a big window at either end of it. Its
dark panelled walls were hung with paintings and
the polished wood floor was covered with fine
silk carpets. The furniture was dark and solid and
the chairs deep and comfortable. There were two
people in the room; an elderly man, white-haired
and as outsize as his son, and a small plump
lady with a pretty face and dark hair only just
beginning to turn grey. She appeared considerably younger than her husband and was dressed
with great elegance; she came hurrying across the

room to embrace her son and greet Jenny and Oliver with a charm devoid of curiosity. Jenny liked her; she liked the Professor's father too. He had blue twinkling eyes and a slow smile which put her at her ease at once as Mevrouw van Draak te Solendijk sat her down on an outsize sofa, sat down beside her, made room for Oliver to settle between them, and began a pleasant undemanding conversation.

The Professor hadn't said much when he had introduced them, but presently he interrupted the talk he was having with his father to ask: 'Shall I let Truus know that there will be three more for lunch, Mama?' And Jenny made haste to say: 'Oh, please—it's awfully kind of you, but we simply can't. . .'

The Professor ignored this and his mother smiled at her nicely while it was left to his father to say: 'Of course you must stay—we are delighted to meet you and Oliver, my dear, we have heard so much about you. And we don't go out a great deal; if you could bear with our elderly company?'

He was a poppet; perhaps his son would be like that in another three decades or so. . . Jenny blinked rapidly and assured him that they would love to stay.

Several hours later, driving back in the Panther, sitting in the back this time, while Oliver sat proudly beside the driver, Jenny mulled over her afternoon. It had been very pleasant; the Professor might be a bad-tempered, arrogant man, but not with everyone, it seemed. She had seen a different side of him and he had seemed ten years younger. They had lunched at a round table in a richly sombre dining room and Oliver had behaved beautifully. The food had been delicious, served by a cheerful, round-faced girl who called Oliver *schatje* and brought him a special ice-cream in place of the elaborate dessert served to his elders. He had shared Jenny's lemonade too, for the Professor had suggested mildly that after such a crack on the head, anything stronger might give her a headache again. She had agreed so meekly that he had given her a surprised look, this time quite without mockery.

Her thoughts occupied her nicely until they reached Kasteel te Solendijk, while she studied the back of the Professor's head and thought how handsome he was, even from that angle, but they received a severe jolt when she remembered that he was angry with her. He would save his rage until she had quite recovered from her tumble, of course, and then she would get the full force of it. Well, there was no point in dwelling upon it. She closed her eyes and when she opened them again they were almost there.

It was as they were going indoors that she asked him: 'Why doesn't your father live here? This is the family home, isn't it?'

He stopped to answer her. 'Oh, yes—although the house in Amsterdam is a family home too. But it is more convenient for my parents to live there now that they are older—besides, this place is more suitable for a married man with a family.'

Her world spun around her. 'You're married—and a family. . .'

She didn't see the gleam in his eyes. He answered smoothly: 'Not yet.' He held the door open for her and when she was inside: 'I should go and lie down for an hour or two if I were you. I'll take Oliver with me in the car—I've a couple of calls to make.'

'Aunt Bess. . .'

'Leave her to me. Go upstairs like a sensible girl.'

Jenny did as she was told and fell asleep almost at once, to wake an hour or two later, immediately worrying away at the Professor's remark about getting married, so that her rest did her no good at all. She got up at last. A breath of air would clear her head and help her to be her usual sensible self before she dressed for the evening. She tidied herself quickly and went through the house, seeing nobody, although she could hear voices in the drawing room; she was intent on slipping into the garden through a side door. She had it half open when the Professor said from behind her: 'Ah, there you are. . .slipping away. . .'

Jenny was up in arms at once. 'I was not—I

merely wanted to walk in the gardens. How dare you. . .'

He sounded amused. 'My dear girl, how you do take me up!' He took her hand off the door handle and closed the door, and she braced herself. He was going to take the lid off his temper and tell her off for being careless about Oliver. She made herself look at him and said snappily:

'All right, you're bursting to pick holes in me, aren't you, just because Oliver went off like that—well, you don't have to! I know that I shouldn't have let him go out of my sight for one single second, but I don't need you to tell me.'

'I wasn't going to.' His voice was mild.

'Oh, yes, you were!' Her cheeks were indignantly pink by now. 'You were fuming—and how was I supposed to whistle when I'd knocked myself on the head. You—you swore at me and you called me silly. . .' Her voice had risen a little and the desire to burst into tears was so great that she had to stop to gulp them down and found that she couldn't any more. 'I hate you!' she blazed and flew back across the hall and upstairs to her room. She stayed there, pleading a headache through the closed door to Aunt Bess, and refusing the tray sent up to her. What with hunger and weeping she passed a miserable night.

CHAPTER EIGHT

JENNY looked at her pale, puffy-eyed face with
distaste in the morning. She was a fright, and no
make-up could quite disguise her pink nose and
red eyes. She did the best she could and was
thankful to find that only Oliver was at breakfast.
The Professor was leaving the house as she went
down, but beyond giving her a quiet good morning as he shut his house door, he had nothing
to say.

Aunt Bess had, though. Surveying her from
her bed where she was enjoying breakfast, she
observed. 'You've been bawling your eyes out.
Janet, and I should like to know why. If you're
still fussing about Oliver's little adventure yesterday, you may forget it—no one attaches the least
blame to you.'

'Oh, yes they do,' cried Jenny. 'Professor van
Draak was beastly—you have no idea! I wish I'd
never come—I wish Margaret had come instead
of me in the first place, then perhaps he'd be
better tempered.'

Her aunt buttered toast with deliberation. 'You
think that Eduard—and I do wish you would stop

calling him Professor in that absurd fashion—is pining for her?'

She obviously wanted an answer. 'Well, Oliver said. . .and I saw them together at Dimworth. . .I mean, Aunt Bess, it's rather hard on him that I'm here and not Margaret. He's not had much chance she's very pretty and someone will marry her sooner or later.'

'I should have thought that he had had a very good chance; he is rich, successful and good-looking—everything Margaret considers important in life. However, I do see what you mean.' Aunt Bess looked thoughtful and a little crafty. 'But there's no point in this discussion, is there, Jenny? And we shall be going home in a few days now. Eduard has asked me to stay for a further day or so and I've told him that we shall be delighted to do so. I should like the opportunity of seeing something of the country again and he would like me to meet his parents. A pity that his brother and sisters are away.'

'Brother and sisters?' repeated Jenny, just like a parrot. 'I didn't know that he had any—he doesn't look the kind of man to have any family at all. I was surprised to find that he had a mother and father. . .'

'Don't be absurd, Janet. There are three sisters and one brother, all younger than he,' said Aunt Bess briskly. 'The brother is at present in Ottawa—he is also a doctor, on some course or

other. His three sisters are all married, two of
them are living in Friesland, the youngest is travelling with her husband in France.'

'Well, I never!' muttered Jenny. Somehow the
fact that the Professor was the eldest of quite a
large family gave her a different idea of him; she
had always thought of him as being withdrawn
and solitary, and here he was in the bosom of a
loving home circle. Her thoughts were interrupted
by her aunt.

'I shall get up now and we will go for a drive.
I feel very well, although I shall be glad to know
the results of all those tests. Supposing we go to
Scheveningen? We could have lunch there and
Oliver can do his shopping.' She pushed the
bedtable away from her. 'Now go along, my dear,
and keep him amused until I'm ready.'

Jenny had been gone quite a few minutes
before Miss Creed lifted the telephone receiver
beside her bed and asked for an English number.

Scheveningen was fun, even though Jenny saw
Eduard van Draak's face wherever she looked. If
this was being in love, she thought morosely, then
the quicker she found a cure for it, the better.
They had lunch at the Corvette in the Kurhaus,
a lively, noisy place which delighted Oliver and
made conversation of a serious nature well-nigh
impossible, which from Jenny's point of view
was very satisfactory. And after lunch Aunt Bess
stayed in the car while she and Oliver went to

the shops to buy a present for his mother.

There were a great many things to choose from, but his choice fell on a gaudy table lamp in the shape of a Dutch girl in costume which, when the right button was pressed, played 'The Bluebells of Scotland'. It cost a good deal more money than he possessed and Jenny obliged with the difference, inwardly uneasy as to its reception by Margaret. But surely she would realise that Oliver found it a splendid gift and at least pretend to like it?

They bore the thing back to the car and unwrapped it to show Aunt Bess, who gazed at it with a wooden face before remarking warmly: 'Why, Oliver, what a lovely present—just what your mother would like to have. Did you choose it all by yourself?' She gave him an unexpected kiss. 'Clever boy! Now we will return to Kasteel te Solendijk and have our tea, I hink.'

Jenny and Oliver were in the drawing room, trying out the lamp's raucous tune, when the Professor returned home. He flung the door wide with a thunderous face and a: 'What on earth...?' and Jenny could have hugged him for his swift: 'That's something quite out of the ordinary—is it for your mother, Oliver?'

The little boy looked at him anxiously. 'Do you like it?' he enquired. 'I chose it myself, and Jenny says Mummy will love it because I found it specially or her.'

'Jenny is quite right—presents chosen for

someone you love are always doubly precious. Shall we have that tune again?'

He got down on his knees beside the child and listened to 'The Bluebells of Scotland' again, and when it was finished spoke to Jenny for the first time. Delightful, isn't it? Have you had a good day?' His voice was polite and formal.

'Yes, thank you. Aunt Bess enjoyed herself very much—I think it did her good. She's resting now.' Equally polite, she added: 'I hope you had a good day too.'

His blue eyes swept over her. 'Not particularly.' He got to his feet, towering over the pair of them. 'I have some work to do, I'm afraid, but I shall see you dinner.' He bent to ruffle Oliver's hair. 'If you're in bed by seven o'clock, I'll come and say goodnight.'

The room seemed very quiet after he had gone. After a moment Oliver said: 'Isn't he super, Jenny?'

'Yes, my lamb.' It was lovely to be able to admit it to someone who would never know just how she felt. 'Now if you're to be in bed and tucked up we'd better wrap this up and go upstairs. You can say goodnight to Aunt Bess on the way.'

Jenny dressed with great care that evening, putting on the pink dress she had worn on the cruise; it was a little grand perhaps, but even she, a girl with no conceit of herself, was aware that she looked quite lovely in it. And she piled her hair, too, in shining rolls and coils which took a long time but was well worth it. At least her appearance boosted her *amour propre* and she went down the beautiful old staircase with her chin well up, touching the polished rail with her fingers as she went, humming a little under her breath. It was a pity that there was no one to see her beautifully groomed and gowned and without, seemingly, a care in the world. She executed a few dance steps as she went and then stopped abruptly, for there was someone to see her after all; the Professor leaning against an enormous pillow cupboard against a shadowy wall. He came forward to wait for her at the foot of the staircase.

'Don't stop on my account,' he begged her silkily, 'or was it on my account?'

Jenny came running down the last few steps and then, too vexed to look where she was going, tripped on the last step. He put out a hand and set her on her feet again with an amused chuckle which made her grind her teeth. 'I believe you lie in wait for me!' she accused him, and when he said: 'Of course I do,' stood looking up at him, her mouth open. 'Why?' she managed.

The arm that had saved her from falling was still round her shoulders. She felt it tighten and saw how right his eyes were. 'I think I shall take Aaron Hill's advice—"Grasp it like a man of mettle. . ."'

'I am not a nettle,' she protested.

He smiled so that her heart rocked in her chest. 'No, you're as soft as silk, Jenny. . .' He broke off to listen to the sudden commotion at the door and the argent banging of the knocker, but he didn't move to open it, nor did he loose her, but waited while Hans rod across the hall to answer the summons.

Margaret made a dramatic entry. Jenny, quite bewildered at her sudden appearance, yet had the time to wonder unkindly if she had rehearsed it on the way. Certainly it was very effective— effective enough to take the Professor's arm from her shoulders and send him to the door where Margaret had paused, trooping, to cry at exactly the right moment: Eduard, oh, Eduard—I've been in an agony of worry! My darling child kidnapped. . .' She struck another attitude and looked at Jenny. 'How could you!' she uttered. 'I thought better of you, Jenny—I thought you loved my Oliver, and to leave him alone in that manner—a defenceless little boy. . .'

Jenny took a couple of steps forward. 'Whatever are you talking about, Margaret?' and then she made the mistake of adding: 'Who told you, anyway?'

'Ah, so you don't deny it!' Margaret turned to the Professor and caught his coat sleeve and gave it a tug. And he won't like that, thought Jenny, and wisely held her tongue.

'This is an unexpected pleasure, Margaret,' remarked the Professor, and gently removed her hand from his jacket. 'But I don't think I quite understand. Oliver is quite well and safe, you know—if he hadn't been I should have made it my business to let you know immediately.'

Margaret was one of the few girls Jenny knew whose eyes could, at will, be made to swim with tears without in the least detracting from her appearance. They swam now as she lifted them to Eduard's face.

'You didn't want me to know because you felt that you should shield Jenny—I can understand that because you're a man who helps lame dogs. . .'

A flicker of emotion passed over his face. Jenny wasn't near enough to be sure what it had been—mirth, anger. . .it didn't matter, anyway. She said in a matter-of-fact voice: 'Margaret, I'm not sure why you've come, but there was no need—Oliver got separated from me in Amsterdam, but he was perfectly all right and we found him again within a couple of hours, none the worse.' She looked at the Professor. 'That's true, isn't it?'

'Perfectly true. Margaret, who told you about it?'

'Aunt Bess. She telephoned me this morning— quite early. I got Toby to drive me to Gatwick and got on to the first plane I could. There's a taxi out side—you'll pay him?'

The Professor nodded to Hans, standing like a statue in the background, and he slid silently outside to come back presently with two suitcases.

The Professor glanced at them with an expression less face. 'Take them up to the Blue Room, will you Hans, and ask Hennie to see if Oliver is still awake.' If he is he will want to come down and see his mother. He turned back to Margaret. 'Come into the drawing-room I'm sure you could do with a drink while we explain exactly what happened. Miss Creed will be down presently.'

Margaret allowed herself to be led across the hall and as they passed her, the Professor said: 'You too, Jenny.'

Margaret sank into a chair with a grace Jenny frankly envied, and looked around her. 'How I've longed to see your home,' she murmured, and then: Could someone unpack for me? I must change for dinner, mustn't I, but I'll be very quick so that you need only put it back for a short time.'

The Professor was either very deeply in love or perhaps it was his beautiful manners, for he said at once: 'Of course we will put dinner back for you, but do see Oliver first, then you will feel completely reassured.'

He was standing with his back to the great fireplace and Jenny had taken a chair facing the door. It was flung open almost immediately and

Oliver, in his dressing gown and slippers, rushed in, clutching his present.

'Mummy,' he cried, 'why are you here? You haven't come to take me back to Dimworth, have you? I'm having a simply super time!'

He allowed himself to be embraced at some length and then pushed his parcel on to his mother's knee. I've brought you a present, I chose it. . .'

Margaret looked at it without much interest. 'How lovely, darling. I'll open it later.'

'Now, please, Mummy,' he beseeched her.

He helped her to take off the layers of paper and the doll was revealed, and before Margaret could say anything, he pressed the button and then stood back listening to the tinny little tune, his small chest thrust out with pride. His mother pushed it away so sharply that it fell to the ground and the tune stopped abruptly. 'Darling, it's lovely, but what would I do with it, for heaven's sake?'

He had gone white, his eyes enormous, his small mouth buttoned tight against tears. 'You broke it,' he said. 'You don't like it. . .'

He turned away and hid his head in Jenny's skirts and she said in her soft, comforting voice: 'It was an accident, my lamb. Mummy's tired—she came hurrying all that long way to see you. Look, we'll pick it up and tomorrow we'll find someone to mend it—it'll be as good as new and you can give it to her again.'

His small lip quivered as he stared at her.
'Honour bright?'

'Honour bright.' She looked across at the
Professor wishing that he would do something—
anything but just stand there, looking as though
he were watching a play, but now he spoke.

'I know just the man who will put it right,
Oliver—shall I take it with me tomorrow and get
him to see to it. It was only a little fall, you
know.' He had bent to collect the lamp and was
holding it in his hand. 'Look, the doll's all right,
it's only the tune.' He smiled at the little boy,
a gentle, kind smile which Jenny found very
disturbing, and Oliver, reassured, said quite
cheerfully:

'Oh, will you please find the man and let him
put it right?' and when Jenny gave him a little
push towards his silent mother, he went to her
and kissed her cheek and said: 'I didn't know
you were tired Mummy, truly I didn't,' and submitted to her embrace once more, and when the
Professor suggested: 'What about bed, old chap?'
he nodded and said goodnight. Only at the door
he turned round to ask Jenny if she would go up
presently and tuck him up.

She found him in bed five minutes later, tears
pouring down his cheeks; it took her ten minutes
to quieten him and another ten to get him to sleep.
She went downstairs again, wishing that she could

have gone to her room and stayed there for the rest of the evening and wondering why Aunt Bess had telephoned to Margaret. What could she have said to make her some tearing over to Holland as though Oliver were an grave danger? Unless she had used it as an excuse—after all, she had wanted to come in the first place, and anxiety or not, she had found time to pack two large suitcases before she left.

The Professor was still in the drawing room, a glass in his hand, looking perfectly calm and collected, and Aunt Bess was with him.

'Oliver was a little upset,' explained Jenny, accepting her glass and sitting down near her aunt. 'Aunt Bess, why did you tell Margaret?'

Miss Creed sought out a lorgnette from the various chains dangling down her front and levelled it at Jenny. 'Are you presuming to criticise me, Janet? I merely mentioned it in the course of conversation—she chose to put the wrong construction upon my remarks that is entirely her own fault. Eduard has explained everything very nicely, though; she quite understands that it was absolutely no fault of yours, and as I pointed out to her, if she had been in charge in the child, she would probably have had hysterics and been of no use whatsoever. That's a pretty dress do you not think so, Eduard?'

Jenny was aware that she was being studied at some length. 'Very charming,' murmured their host laconically—and only half an hour ago he had told her that she was as soft as silk. . . She took care not to look at him and made polite conversation until Margaret quite lovely in blue chiffon, came in, begging every one's pardon for being late and keeping them waiting and accepted a drink from the Professor with a smile which made Jenny seethe and ask: 'Is Oliver asleep?'

Margaret turned to look at her. 'Oliver? I don't know—I didn't look.' She smiled quite sweetly at Jenny; she had accused her of negligence and carelessness such a short time ago, but she had already forgotten about it, just as she would have dismissed as unimportant the little episode with the lamp. She tucked a hand into the Professor's arm and said prettily: 'I'm simply famished!'

The evening was hers, of course. Aunt Bess said very little, surprisingly enough, and although Jenny joined in the talk when someone addressed her, she made no attempt to focus any interest upon herself. The Professor didn't say much either, but he looked at Margaret a great deal and when she suggested that she would like to see something of Holland, offered to drive her to one or two places of interest. Madly in love, Jenny decided sadly. She had thought, for the briefest of moments, when they had been in the hall together. . . But now Margaret was here; he had been amusing himself with that silly talk about nettles.

Aunt Bess went to bed quite early after dinner, declaring that her outing had tired her more than she had supposed. 'And you might come with me, Jenny,' she requested. 'I'm getting slow.'

So Jenny had gone upstairs too, willingly enough, because to sit with the two of them for the rest of the evening was rather more than she could bear; better to go to her own room and wonder what they were saying to each other.

Surprisingly, the Professor was at breakfast in the morning, and when he suggested that she might like to accompany him and Margaret to Leiden she was tempted to agree, especially as he had included Oliver in the invitation, but Margaret, smiling sweetly, declared that if he went, she wouldn't be able to bear his chatter. 'The darling gives me such a headache,' she explained plaintively, 'and I haven't got over that nightmare journey.'

So Jenny said that she would stay home with Oliver. There was plenty to do, she declared enthusiastically, and as they would be leaving Holland soon now, it was a pity to miss the chance of going somewhere.

'Such as where?' asked her host gently, and when he didn't answer: 'The final results of the tests should be ready tomorrow,' he pointed out. 'I believe Miss Creed plans to return to Dimworth as soon as possible once they are known. I thought a small farewell lunch, so that Oliver might join us.'

Margaret agreed enthusiastically, but he wasn't looking at her. He was watching Jenny, who, well aware of it, refused to look him in the eye but addressed a point over his left shoulder. 'I'm sure that will be very nice,' she said sedately. 'Oliver will love it. And now if you'll excuse us. . . Oliver, we'll go and find Aunt Bess and see if we may borrow Dobbs and the car.'

'There's a Mini eating its head off in the garage,' suggested her host, 'why not borrow it?' He was gathering up his letters and not looking at her. 'You might drive to Leiden and meet us for lunch.'

'How kind, but actually we've been wanting to go to Alkmaar—it's the cheese market today and Oliver is very keen to see it.' She turned a speaking eye upon the boy as she spoke, giving him a warning look which he understood at once, for it wasn't the first time. . . The Professor sat back in his chair, apparently blind to this byplay, receiving this mendacious statement with a bland expression which gave nothing away.

'Oh, well, in that case,' he said carelessly, 'take the Mini to Alkmaar. The market is great fun.' His tone implied that the fun was strictly for children and tourists.

'Where are you and Mummy going?' asked Oliver.

'Er—the Tropical Museum, the Pilgrim Fathers' House and possibly the Museum of Antiquities.'

'I think cheese sounds more fun.'

The Professor didn't answer this, only smiled.

Aunt Bess, invited to go to Alkmaar, declined. 'Tourists,' she sniffed, 'eating ices and gaping. Go and enjoy yourselves. I shall probably go into den Haag with Dobbs presently for some last-minute shopping. Janet, I shall decide today when we are to return.'

'Will Mummy come with us?' Oliver wanted to know.

Miss Creed gave him a searching look. 'And why do you ask, Oliver?'

'She said she was going to marry the Professor. If does, where will I go?' He looked so forlorn that Jenny plucked him off his feet and hugged him close.

'With Mummy, of course—won't he, Aunt Bess?'

But before that lady could reply, he protested: 'But I don't want him for a daddy. He's my friend. . . Jenny, if he married you instead, I could come and stay with you here, couldn't I?'

Jenny frowned ferociously and went a bright pink, but her voice was quite matter-of-fact. 'Well, love, that wouldn't really do—if Mummy and the Professor want to get married, they'd hardly want to marry someone else, would they?'

'You've gone very red,' observed Oliver.

'That's because I'm out of breath hugging you. Say goodbye to Aunt Bess and we'll go and find that Mini.'

The Panther de Ville had gone by the time they reached the garage, but Dobbs was there, talking to Hans, and polishing the car.

'The little car's all ready, Miss Jenny,' he told her, and I was to tell you to be sure and be back by tea time.'

'Oh, indeed,' Jenny tossed her mane of hair over her shoulders. 'I can't think why. We shall stay until we've seen everything we intend to—and you can tell Professor van Draak so.'

'Well, I'm sure I don't know, Miss Jenny,' protested Dobbs in a fatherly way, 'but I do know that I'd rather not cross him—a very nice gentleman, but likes his own way, so to speak.' He nodded to himself. 'Quite right and proper too.'

'That's as may be,' said Jenny obscurely as she settled Oliver beside her and drove off.

There was a great deal to see in Alkmaar. They arrived before the cheese market opened, which gave them time to have their elevenses in a little café in the main street and then wander down its length, peering at the shop windows. And when they reached the Waaggebouw they joined the group of sightseers, to watch the little figures moving round the clock tower as it struck the hour. It was only a firm promise to return and view this phenomenon as many times as possible that persuaded Oliver to leave and enter the cheese market.

Here the teams of white-clad porters in their gay boaters, carrying their enormous trays of cheeses, caught his fancy, so that they spent the rest of the morning there, sampling the cheese, buying highly coloured postcards and talking to any number of English and American tourists. Aunt Bess would have hated it, Jenny decided, prising Oliver away from a large family of children with the promise of lunch.

They went to the Schuyt restaurant on the Stationsplein and had a splendid meal; not perhaps well balanced, but very satisfying, especially for Oliver, who was of an age to enjoy *potat frites* with mustard pickles, followed by a enormous ice, rainbow-hued and smothered in whipped cream. They were strolling away from this repast, trying to decide whether to find the house with the cannon ball still in its wall—a relic of the Spanish Occupation—or go back for another sight of the figures prancing round the clock tower, when Jenny's suggestion that there was ample time to do both decided them to go in search of the cannon ball first, so they started off in its general direction.

But once over the bridge at the end of the main street they became quite lost. But it was a small town and they hadn't strayed far and there was plenty to look at as they wandered along. They found the house at last, paid their admission and started up the narrow little staircase. There were two or three rooms on each landing, all furnished in the style of a bygone age. Oliver, completely enraptured, peered and explored, begging Jenny to look at a dozen things at a time. 'Cheese, and now this!' he exclaimed ecstatically, and went on to the little landing to peer over the rail at the head of the stairs. 'Someone's coming up,' he informed her, and then gave a great shout. 'Professor van Draak—did you mean to come? How did you know we were here? Where's Mummy?'

'At Solendijk.' The Professor reached the tiny landing now and it was impossible for Jenny to pretend that he wasn't there.

She asked, not allowing her gaze to wander from the baby's cradle she was studying: 'Didn't she want to come?'

He was right beside her, because there was really nowhere else for him to go. 'Er—no.' And when she looked at him at last, he stared down his splendid nose at her and added: 'I have a patient here—I remembered that I had arranged to see her doctor. Margaret isn't interested in patients.' He added blandly: 'We had a delightful morning in Leiden.'

'And have you seen your patient's doctor?' asked Jenny, keeping to the point.

'Oh, yes—I did so before he started his afternoon surgery.'

'What a pity that you had to cut short your outing with Margaret.'

'I must agree, but then I had the happy idea of finding the pair of you so that we might finish our outings in company.'

'What about Margaret?' persisted Jenny doggedly.

'I think she had had sufficient of Leiden by lunch time—we had a meal in the town.' He smiled at her, his manner still bland. 'Such a charming and pretty woman.'

It was on the tip of her tongue to ask him why, if he found Margaret so fascinating, he hadn't rushed back to keep her company, but all she said was: 'Actually, she's beautiful.'

Oliver had been roaming round during their conversation. Now he declared that he had seen everything and was ready to go downstairs again. 'Perhaps we could have an ice?' he asked hopefully.

'We've only just had lunch,' Jenny said, so crossly that he looked quite startled and the Professor made haste to say: 'Shall we compromise with coffee and a glass of lemonade? there's a delightful coffee shop quite close by.'

Jenny made one more effort. 'Oughtn't you to go back?' she asked. 'I mean, haven't you any patients to see?'

He gave her an austere look. 'I am enjoying a rare free day—although enjoying isn't perhaps the right word.'

'Oh, I'm sorry.' She felt all at once mean and petty. 'I didn't mean to be horrid. Look, would you like to take Oliver with you, and I'll potter off on my own.'

His sudden smile warmed her to her very heart. 'Oh, Jenny, what a darling you are—why didn't we meet years ago?'

She stood speechless. He liked her after all, perhaps more than that—but he loved Margaret. Margaret had told her so, or at least, she corrected herself, she had said that she was going to marry him. Perhaps they had quarrelled and he had rushed off seeking consolation. She said in a sensible voice: 'Let's go and have some coffee and Oliver could choose what he wants to do next.' She smiled up at the blue eyes staring so hard at her. 'After all, it's his day.'

'I think it's my day too,' said the Professor thoughtfully.

They spent a riotous afternoon; there was a small *kermis*, a fair, tucked away behind the main street and the three of them tried each one of its attractions, and when they were tired of that, wandered round the booths, Jenny and Oliver licking large ice-cream cones while their companion contented himself with his pipe. But he did try his hand at the shooting gallery and won a hideous toy dog, its nylon fur a brilliant blue which Oliver found irresistible, and to equal things up, as he put it, he purchased a bead necklace for Jenny. She hung it round her neck and admired it at length, knowing that she would keep the gaudy thing for the rest of her life.

They were standing together watching Oliver whirling round on an old-fashioned roundabout, when he said abruptly: 'You were lying, weren't you?' Jenny gave him a wary look, aware that she had lied to him on several occasions. 'I asked you if you disliked me,' he went on, 'and you told me that you did. That wasn't—isn't—true, is it?'

Perhaps it was the carnival atmosphere around them, or just the intoxication of being with him, that made her answer recklessly. 'No, it wasn't true. I didn't—don't dislike you, though perhaps I did at first. I don't know any more. . .you are rather arrogant, you know, only I've got used to that now.'

His eyes were on her face. 'I'm not a young man—perhaps too old to marry.'

'Oh, nonsense!' she cried warmly. 'Of course you're not too old. Besides, Margaret is thirty—only ten years younger than you.'

'Margaret?' There was a wry amusement in his voice so that she hurried on:

'She seems much younger than that, but that's because she's so pretty, but she's really quite good at running a big household. Aunt Bess only does it because she prefers to live in Scotland with her parents besides, all her friends live there.'

'Giving me Dutch courage, Jenny?'

She didn't look at him because if she did she wasn't sure what she might say. 'I don't think you need it—only you've got this silly notion about being too old for a wife and children.'

'You think that I would make a good husband?' He sounded only a little interested.

'Oh, yes—and think how you could fill that lovely old house of yours with children. And there are the dogs, of course, and the cat—and you could have a donkey for the little ones and a pony for them to ride later. . .'

'Are we talking in dozens?' he wanted to know, and this time there was a laugh in his voice.

Jenny had a sudden vivid picture of Kasteel te Solendijk's old walls ringing to the shouts of little boys with bright blue eyes and haughty noses. There would be little girls too, of course—perhaps with coppery hair? She said soberly: 'It's a house that needs children.'

'Well, there's Oliver for a start, though I hardly think that Margaret would marry on his account.'

'Well, I don't know about that—he needs a father, doesn't he, or an uncle or something. He'll inherit Dimworth when he's eighteen, but that's a long way to go.' She moved a little away from him. 'Here's Oliver now—I should think he must be tired out.'

Oliver declared that he wasn't tired at all, but he agreed willingly enough to the Professor's proposal that they should return home. 'But only if I may drive with you,' he declared.

The big man smiled down at him, 'Certainly you may,' and turned to Jenny. But she firmly refused his offer of a lift in his car and was indignant when he said mildly: 'Oh, dear—and I have already arranged for a garage to pick up the Mini and bring it down tomorrow.'

'Well, really!' she burst out. 'Of all the high-handed. . .'

'It is my car,' he reminded her silkily. 'Besides, I can't possibly drive and answer Oliver's inevitable questions at the same time.'

'He could have come with me.'

'He said he wanted to come with me. It is his day—you said so yourself.'

She choked back temper. 'Do you think I can't drive or something?'

'My dear girl, I would never have allowed you to drive the Mini if I had supposed that.'

She stood, muttering crossly until he said: 'I've enjoyed my afternoon—makebelieve, of course, but shall we not spoil it by quarrelling?'

She asked in a small voice: 'What do you mean—makebelieve?'

'Just that—doing something; being someone one wishes to be and cannot.' He added: 'At least for the moment.'

He sounded resigned and a little remote and her temper fled before a wave of love. 'It wasn't all makebelieve,' she assured him. 'I meant what I said—that I don't dislike you.'

She smiled up at him, her lovely eyes warm and soft. She hadn't meant to say that, but her truant tongue had had the last word. But she was quite unprepared when his arms caught her close, 'No, it wasn't makebelieve, Jenny,' and he didn't sound remote or resigned, 'and this isn't either.' He kissed her hard and lingeringly and then let her go without a word as Oliver, at last sated with the pleasures of the *kermis*, came trotting towards them.

CHAPTER NINE

THERE was nothing makebelieve about Margaret's face when they got back. She had too indolent a nature to be deeply angry about anything, but she had a decidedly pettish expression which quite marred her lovely features. She was sitting on the lawn as they drove up the drive and round the side to the garages with Oliver—for a great treat—sitting on the Professor's knee, steering the car. Jenny waved and called to her as they passed and received nothing but a cross look in return. In all fairness to Margaret, she had to admit that had she been in her shoes, she would have been more than just cross, although the expedition that afternoon had been innocent enough. She corrected herself—not quite innocent; there had been their conversation and the Professor had kissed her with a good deal of feeling, probably because he had wanted to kiss Margaret, who wasn't there.

When they reached the garage she got out with a murmured excuse and hurried into the house. Oliver had refused to go with her and she supposed that if the Professor wanted Margaret to himself, he would think up something to occupy the small boy. She went to her aunt's room first, but Miss Creed wasn't here, so she went slowly to her own room and sat down on the bed, wondering how best to keep out of the Professor's and Margaret's way until dinner time. A wasted exercise as it turned out, for standing by the window later on, idly looking out, she saw the Panther pass under her window. The Professor was driving and Margaret was beside him; both of them were dressed for the evening.

Jenny went downstairs to look for Aunt Bess then, and found her in the library, a lofty apartment smelling of leather and books and furnished with a number of deep armchairs, each with its own table and lamp. Aunt Bess was sitting at her ease, browsing through some old bound volumes of *Punch*, but she glanced up as Jenny went in.

'There you are,' she observed unnecessarily. 'Oliver is having his bath before his supper this evening—he's with Hennie. Eduard has taken Margaret to see some friends of his. Probably they won't be back until the small hours. That leaves you and me—we can discuss our journey home in peace.'

'Yes, Aunt Bess.' Jenny strove to make her voice interested and cheerful, with so little success that her companion said: 'Down in the dumps again! You'll be glad to get back to Dimworth, I dare say.'

Jenny said that she would, which was partly

true. She wouldn't have to watch Margaret charming Eduard then; at the same time she wouldn't see him, full stop. She couldn't win either way.

'Has he come up to scratch?' asked Aunt Bess vulgarly.

'Who do you mean? Who with?'

'Margaret, of course.'

'I—I don't know, perhaps this evening. . .' Jenny voice trailed off.

'Bah!' exclaimed Miss Creed in ringing tones. 'He won't, you know—not what he wants at all.' She looked sly and changed the subject abruptly. 'I'm going to Amsterdam in the morning to have lunch with Eduard's people, but I'll be back before tea—the tests will be completed by then. I shall go home anyway.' She picked up *Punch* once more. 'Find a book,' she commanded.

So Jenny sat leafing through *Country Life* and several Dutch magazines which she couldn't make head or tail of until it was time to change for the evening. There was no sign of the Professor or of Margaret. She went upstairs to say goodnight to Oliver and then, after a fruitless suggestion that there as really no need for them to change their dress, to her room, to put on a rather sober dress which she had never liked. It was a silk flowered print in beige which did nothing for her at all, and she scraped back her hair in a style to match its dull cut before flouncing downstairs to the drawing room to find Aunt Bess, resplendent in purple and gold chains, waiting for her glass of sherry.

Dinner was delicious, but then all the meals in the Professor's house were; but she pecked at her food as though it were yesterday's porridge, saying 'Yes, Aunt' and 'No, Aunt' with a sad lack of interest in the topic under discussion. She emerged from a gloomy reverie to hear Aunt Bess observe:

'So that is settled—tomorrow evening on the night boat. Eduard must get us cabins. I shall telephone Toby in the morning and tell him to expect us, and you may telephone Florrie after dinner, Janet.'

Jenny said: 'Yes, Aunt Bess,' once again and played with her trifle. It was very short notice, but then Aunt Bess always did what she wanted when she wanted. Somehow or other there would be cabins put at her disposal and however inconvenient her unexpected arrival might be, Dimworth would be ready to receive her.

She telephoned Dimworth as soon as they had had their coffee, using the telephone in the small sitting room because Aunt Bess didn't wish to be disturbed in the drawing room, and listened to Florrie worriedly telling her that they would be ready for Miss Creed when she arrived. 'Though mind you, Miss Jenny,' said Florrie's soft Somerset voice, 'there's the carpet in Miss

Creed's room being shampooed and if it will be ready in time, I'm sure I don't know—and us run out of jam for the visitors and a nasty leak in the south wing.'

'Don't worry,' Jenny told her, 'Aunt Bess is going to be too tired to notice anything. I daresay she'll go straight to bed.'

'Who is going straight to bed?' asked the Professor from behind her and she turned round to see him stand aside in the doorway so that Margaret might come into the room too. He looked so pleased with himself that Jenny's hand shook a little on the receiver—and Margaret looked radiant. There was no other word to describe the look on her face—or perhaps a cat who had licked the cream pot empty. . .

She explained woodenly: 'Aunt Bess thinks she should go back to Dimworth. She's quite confident that the tests are OK, but even if they're not, she's going. . .she asked me to telephone our housekeeper.'

Margaret cast herself down on a deep crimson sofa, an excellent foil for her blonde beauty. 'Well, I shan't go,' she declared petulantly, 'just as everything is marvellous. . . You can take Oliver with you, Jenny—I'll come home later.' She turned to her host, still standing at the door. 'Eduard, you'll let me stay?'

His ready: 'Of course, my dear,' cut Jenny like a knife. She said, still very wooden: 'Yes, of course we'll take Oliver with us.' She forced herself to look at the Professor. 'I hope you don't think us rude and ungrateful, leaving so unexpectedly. . .'

'But your aunt had already told me,' he said cheerfully, 'provided of course that I get a good report from the hospital tomorrow, and the final decision to leave does rest with me. . . She is lunching with my parents tomorrow, isn't she? The Mini will be back in the morning. Would you and Oliver like to have it so that you can have a last fling together?'

Jenny never wanted to see the Mini again; she thanked him nicely but with some coolness, whereupon he asked her if she would prefer to borrow the Bristol 412 which he occasionally used in place of the Panther. 'It's a fast car,' he pointed out, 'if you found the Mini too slow, but very safe.'

She declined that too and was murmuring a few well-chosen words before getting herself out of the room, when he remarked casually: 'There is a donkey arriving in the morning, by the way— Oliver might like a ride on her. I'm buying a pony too, but he won't arrive until a week or so. You see I took your advice, Jenny.'

'How nice, I'm sure Oliver will love that.' She was aware that her voice was too high and turned with relief to the forgotten receiver in her hand; Florrie's voice was still rambling on, a little doubtfully now because she was getting no reply, so Jenny explained and rang off, anxious to be gone. But she was delayed once more, this time by Margaret.

'What time shall we go tomorrow?' she asked the Professor, and smiled at Jenny as she spoke. 'I'm so excited I feel exhausted; I simply must have a good night's rest.'

'One o'clock?' he suggested. 'I'll come and fetch you. No, that won't do, because I must see Miss Creed before she leaves. You will have to be fetched, but that will present no difficulties—I'll telephone presently. Margaret, are you going to tell Jenny?'

'No, certainly not! It's my lovely secret—well, it's your secret too, I suppose, and don't you dare to say a word.' She got up and stretched languidly. 'I'm off to bed—I must pack an overnight bag, I suppose.' She smiled again at Jenny: 'Wouldn't you like to know?' she murmured, and leaned up to kiss the Professor's cheek before sauntering to the door.

'I must go too,' said Jenny urgently. 'I promised I'd pack for Aunt Bess.'

It was a pity that he was standing in the doorway and showed no sign of moving. 'Not in the least curious, Jenny?'

'Well, of course I am,' she snapped, 'but don't think you can tease me into asking questions, because I'm not going to—besides, I can guess.'

'You might guess wrong.' He was smiling down at her, looking amused. 'You're very ill-tempered this evening. I thought that after this afternoon. . . That dress doesn't suit you, either.'

'It's a perfectly good dress,' she told him sharply, 'and this afternoon was makebelieve—you said so yourself.' She remembered how he had kissed her and went red, feeling the tide of colour wash over her face while he stared.

'Ah, so you remember, too,' he said softly. 'There's great deal I want to say to you, Jenny, but you're not in a very receptive mood, are you?' And he stood aside, wishing her goodnight in a voice which held a laugh, so that there was nothing for her to do but go upstairs, to pause outside Aunt Bess's door to gain composure. And once inside she was for once thankful that her aunt kept her busy helping her to bed and then packing for her under her sharp eyes. But presently Aunt Bess observed: 'That will do for the present. Go to bed, child, you look like skimmed milk—you need a good night's rest.'

Something Jenny didn't have.

By the time she and Oliver had breakfasted the donkey had arrived. A kindly Hans offered the information and they went without waste of time to the paddock behind the stables. It was a very small donkey and not in the best condition either, its mild eyes apprehensive as they made much of it, something which worried Jenny until Hans

joined them with the carrots he had gone to fetch;
to explain to her that the Professor had gone to
a great deal of trouble contacting various societies
until he had found one which had a donkey in
need of a good home and at the same time were
willing to transport the little beast without delay.

'But I thought it took weeks. . .'

Hans gave her a tolerant smile! 'It probably
does, miss, but if Professor van Draak makes
up his mind about something, he doesn't regard
obstacles.'

'Oh—Well, yes. A week or two here and she'll
be as fit as a fiddle, won't she? Is the pony coming
from the same place?'

'No, miss. I understand he is a child's—what
is the word?—mount no longer required by the
owner. The Professor intends to buy a second
donkey later on.' He paused to watch Oliver feed-
ing carrots to the donkey. 'Perhaps Oliver would
like a ride?'

So they all went for an amble round the paddock, until Hans gave it his opinion that the
animal would probably be glad of a rest. Oliver
slid off her back at once, saying loudly: 'I shall
come here to stay very often, then I can ride. . .'

'Well, yes, my lamb, but you'll have to. . .'
Jenny stopped. How very complicated life would
be for Oliver if his mother married Eduard. He
wouldn't need to be invited then, of course,
because he would be living at Solendijk. But what

about Dimworth? That was, after all, his true home and inheritance.

'Why don't you finish?' demanded Oliver.

'Oh, I've forgotten what I was going to say—it wasn't anything important.' She caught Hans' eyes upon her and had an uneasy feeling that he had known what she had been thinking and for some reason it amused him—almost as though he knew something she didn't.

'How about elevenses?' she asked, 'and Hans, it's such a mild day, do you suppose we could have a picnic lunch out here by the pool? I'll help carry it out.'

He beamed at her. 'Of course, Miss Wren, and there'll be no need for you to do anything.' His tone was mildly reproving at the suggestion.

They had eaten the last crumb of the delicious sandwiches which Hennie had made for them and drained the lemonade jug dry as the Panther swished up the drive and stopped before the front door. The Professor got out and went into the house, to come out again almost immediately and bend his steps in their direction. He had a glass of beer in one hand and a sandwich in the other and folded his length on to the lawn beside them with a cheerful: 'Hullo—have you enjoyed your morning?'

'Smashing!' declared Oliver. 'I went for a ride on your donkey and she liked it.'

'Good.' The Professor took a huge bite. 'And you, Jenny?'

'Very nice, thank you,' she told him demurely. 'Have you been busy?'

He polished off the rest of the sandwich. 'Yes. The test results are excellent. Miss Creed is in Amsterdam?'

Jenny nodded. 'Yes, but she'll be back before tea. Which reminds me that I still have a mass of packing to do and I'd better go and finish it.' She was kneeling beside him, tidying away the remains of their lunch on to a tray, aware that he was watching her. To break the silence she asked: 'Will Margaret be back before we leave?' She looked at him quickly and then away again. 'Should we say goodbye now?'

He glanced at the paper-thin gold watch on his wrist. 'Hasn't she gone yet? No, she won't be back until after you have left—probably not until tomorrow.' He drank the last of his beer. 'Oliver, you had better go and say goodbye to your mother now—she's to be fetched very shortly.'

The little boy ran off and Jenny got to her feet, anxious not to be alone with the Professor. 'I must go. . .' she began, but he chose to misunderstand her. 'Well, Miss Creed will certainly be safer with a companion on the journey.' He took the tray from her and put it down on the grass again, then tucked a hand under her arm. 'I have a fancy to stroll through the gardens,' he observed

mildly. 'I'm sure you're very quick at packing
and there can't be all that much.' He glanced
down at her. 'I like that blue dress. Did you throw
that flowered thing out of the window?'

She couldn't stop her chuckle. 'Of course not.
I'll give it to someone when I get back, though;
I don't much like it myself.'

She was being led away from the pool, towards
the wide gravel path bordered by early autumn
flowers very aware of his hand on her arm.

'Don't you want to say goodbye to Margaret?'
she asked.

'My dear girl, I shall be seeing her again in a
few hours. Tell me, what do you intend to do
when you return to Dimworth?'

Was he going to meet Margaret, then? Where
were they going together? And hadn't Margaret
said that she had to pack an overnight bag? Jenny
had no answer to the questions rotating round and
round inside her head. She said a little absently:
'Well, I'll stay until the house is closed for the
winter, then I—I suppose I'll look for another
job. Perhaps Queen's would take me back. . .'

'So you have decided not to marry Toby?'

She tossed her bright head. 'I decided that
years ago.'

'You have no other plans? There must be a
number of young men dangling after you.'

He was very anxious to marry her off, she
thought crossly, just because his future was all

nicely settled and rosy. She didn't answer but asked instead, not really meaning to: 'When are you going to get married?'

'Oh, at the earliest possible moment,' he assured her suavely. 'I can't have a donkey and pony eating their heads off for nothing.'

She didn't know whether to laugh or cry. 'But it would be a year or two. . .'

'Ah, yes, but Oliver could keep them in practice, could he not?'

Jenny sighed, a sad little sound she wasn't aware of. 'Yes, of course.' Suddenly being with him wasn't to be borne a moment longer; he would walk here with Margaret and tell her about his day and talk about the children. . . She hoped that Margaret would listen intelligently and take an interest in the children, but perhaps he loved her so much that that wouldn't really matter.

'I must pack,' she said in a desperate little voice, and turned and ran back to the house.

Of course he had been right; she could have packed in ten minutes flat if she had needed to. She managed to spin it out until she heard the car which had come to fetch Margaret had driven away, very late, because Margaret hadn't been ready. She had told Jenny nothing when she had gone to say goodbye, only looked smug and pleased with herself and hinted at a marvellous surprise everyone was going to have very shortly. And when Jenny had tried to persuade her to tell her secret she had shrugged and said in her charming, indolent way: 'Oh, Jenny—not now can't you see I've got my hair to do? You'll know soon enough.'

Jenny wandered over to the window to stare at the lovely gardens spread below her. Well, she knew, didn't she—there was really no need to ask Margaret. She couldn't get away fast enough now, away from the lovely old house, its splendid grounds, the excitement of seeing Eduard every day. . .

She decided that it would be safe to go downstairs now, as the master of the house would be in his study, Oliver she had seen, his hand in Hans', crossing the lawn to take another look at the donkey. She would slip out of the side door behind the sitting room and go and look at the vines, so vastly superior to those at Dimworth.

She had reached the hall when the study door was flung open and the Professor stuck his head out, 'Packed?' he wanted to know carelessly. 'In which case, how about a stroll? We didn't finish the last one, did we? Miss Creed won't be back for another hour.'

Jenny restrained herself from bolting back the way she had come. 'No—no, thank you, I mean, I've still got things to do. . .'

'Such as?'

She stared at him helplessly, quite unable to think of any excuse at all. After a long moment he said smoothly: 'You don't want to, do you, Jenny?' His face had become bleak. 'And you must have a very good idea of what I'm going to say to you.'

She took a step backwards. 'Yes, of course— and I don't want. . .that is, I'd rather not. . .' Her voice trembled. 'Please, Eduard, not now.'

His brows rose. 'Not now? And supposing I should come to Dimworth, would I be allowed to tell you then?'

'I. . .yes.' By then she would be able to smile and congratulate him and wish him happy— Margaret too.

His smile was small and mocking. 'I shall remember that.' He had gone inside and shut the door before she could think of anything to say.

She didn't see him to speak to alone after that. Aunt Bess came back very satisfied with herself received the good news of her test results with an air of I-told-you-so, partook of tea and pronounced herself ready to leave. 'And you, Eduard, what will you do with yourself this evening? Margaret either would not or could not give me any coherent answers to my questions.'

'I have to go back to the hospital presently,' he told her pleasantly, 'and I shall be dining with Margaret.' He looked at Jenny as he spoke, but she pretended not to see.

They left a little later, after at least half an hour of loading luggage on to the car, installing Aunt

Bess on to the back seat, finding Oliver, who had gone to say goodbye to the donkey, and finally taking a farewell of the Professor. He stood outside his front door, large and placid, saying all the right things. The last Jenny saw of him was his huge frame outlined against his lovely home, and she didn't see him very clearly for the tears in her eyes.

Their journey home held no hindrances. How the Professor had managed to get them cabins at such short notice was something Jenny didn't worry about; he was a man who would always get what he wanted. Margaret, for instance.

Back at Dimworth life settled into its old pattern once more; everyone was glad to see them back home and Aunt Bess, almost her former self, found fault with everyone, upset Mrs Thorpe, declared that it was a good thing that she was once more able to hold the reins because the household bills were shocking, and then toured the house, picking holes in everything and everyone. Just like old times, thought Jenny. No mention was made of Margaret and surprisingly she neither wrote nor telephoned for several days. When she did do so it was one morning when Jenny was dusting the doll collection. Aunt Bess took the call and presently swept along to where Jenny was carefully rearranging the exhibits.

'Well, she's done it!' declared Miss Creed in

trumpet-like tones. 'Oliver is to have a new father.'

Jenny dropped her feather duster. 'Oh. I'm glad—when are they to be married?'

'As soon as it can be arranged. Presumably they have made some arrangement regarding Oliver—this is, after all, his home, or will be when he's a man.' Aunt Bess allowed herself a snort. 'Not that Margaret has made much effort to make it home for him. However, that must be gone into later, I suppose. He sounds a sensible type, and since they've known each other in their youth, he understands the situation.'

'Their youth?' asked Jenny, quite at sea.

'Well, yes, child. This Dirk van something or other was in Scotland for several years—he knew Margaret long before she met Oliver and married him. Now they have met again and have decided to marry. It seems a splendid arrangement.'

'Where did they meet? I mean, for the second time.' Jenny's voice was almost a whisper so that Aunt Bess begged her to speak up.

'He's a friend of Eduard, strangely enough. Eduard discovered that they knew each other and arranged to take Margaret to see Dirk what's-his-name. They practically fell into each other's arms.' She marched to the door. 'Don't forget the clock,' she said severely as she went out.

Jenny ignored the clock and the remainder of the dolls, too. So Eduard hadn't been in love with

Margaret at all—so what had he wanted to tell her? She remembered how she had run away and begged him not to say any more. She picked up an exact replica of Queen Victoria and gave her a perfunctory dust. 'Fool fool,' she told herself loudly, 'he thinks you don't give a damn—I let him think that, and how on earth am I ever going to find out if it was me?' Her muddled thoughts gave way to several wild ideas, none of them feasible. She could of course go to Holland, but she would have to have a reason. . .'And I'll find one!' she cried fiercely, flung down her duster and flew upstairs to her room, where she locked the door and cried her eyes red.

There were plenty of visitors that afternoon. Jenny watched them straggle through the gate-house, up the broad path to the entrance and went to take her seat behind the big table, loaded with a fresh batch of jam, postcards and brochures. There was a school party, she noted, which meant that Florrie's niece would have to act as guide. The teacher in charge wasn't able to keep them an in order; ever since the time they had discovered a small boy sitting in a priceless William and Mary chair, eating a cheese sandwich, they had had to be careful.

The first few visitors appeared, making straight for the table, as they nearly always did, then armed with a brochure and a bag of sweets, they would wander off to look around them. There was, of course, a hard core of those who didn't know what they wanted, and for that matter, didn't know why they had come in the first place. Jenny pushed her hair off her forehead with a weary hand and opened the petty cash box as the first visitor picked up a handful of cards. One more week, she reflected, then the house would be closed and revert to its glorious winter peace, and she would be free to find a job—or go in search of Eduard. She handed change and wondered just what she would say to him.

An hour later she was still doing a fair trade, although the spate had spent itself and become a steady trickle. She handed a bag of fudge to a small, grubby boy with an engaging grin and gave him back his change with a warm smile and a souvenir pencil for free, and looked up at the next customer.

Eduard. She trembled a little at the sight of him and was furious with herself for it.

'I want to talk to you.' He didn't bother to lower his voice. 'Will you come out from behind that table, Jenny?'

'No.' It would have been little to have said more than that, but she had no breath.

'Then I shall come and sit beside you,' he said blandly, 'and we can talk here.'

'No, certainly not—of course we can't. . .' She gave him a quick glance and saw that he had meant what he had said. Two or three people were approaching, intent on buying postcards; she pressed the floor bell under her foot and hoped that whoever it was detailed to relieve her would come quickly, and watched the door, not looking at him. It was Mrs Thorpe who came bustling in, still wearing the best summer hat, her two-piece covered by a serviceable apron. 'Trouble, dear?' she wanted to know in her penetrating voice.

Jenny avoided answering that. 'I should be glad if you could take over for a little while, Mrs Thorpe—there's something I have to attend to.'

Mrs Thorpe's rather prominent eye had discovered the Professor. 'Why, doctor,' she cried archly and erroneously, 'how delightful to meet you again. No trouble, I hope?'

Jenny admired his suavity as he dealt with the question and added: 'Don't let me keep you from your post, Mrs Thorpe.' His eyes took in the small queue which had formed behind him, but he didn't budge, only looked at Jenny. He wasn't going to move until she went with him and people were beginning to prick up interested ears. She got to her feet and walked round the table and started towards the small arched doorway marked private, and found him right beside her.

She stepped past him as he opened the door and then closed it behind him. The lobby was very small with the circular staircase spiralling up from its centre. Jenny, between staircase and Professor, had no room at all. All the same she asked in a dignified voice, addressing his top waistcoat button: 'What do you want?'

The Professor, probably with an eye to making more room, put his arms around her. 'You, my darling girl, you ridiculous, nettlesome creature, getting silly ideas into your head, taking everything for granted in your usual hoity-toity fashion. You said that if I came to see you here, you would listen to me, so I have come.'

'Well, I can't do anything else, can I?' she pointed out, glad that her voice was so nice and steady although she was very much afraid that in that confined space he would be able to hear her heart beating like a mad thing. And he must have done, for she was caught in a tight embrace and kissed in a purposeful fashion which left her in no doubt whatsoever as to his feelings.

'My dearest dear,' said the Professor lovingly to the top of her head, 'surely you knew that I loved you? Oh, not at once, I must admit, you're bossy and prickly to a fault and everlastingly managing to keep me on tenterhooks—and you're adorable. . .I'm a good deal older than you are, my love, bad-tempered and arrogant too. I shall have to learn to be a good husband, and I will. I promise you, for nothing I have is of any worth unless I have you.'

He bent to kiss her, gently this time. 'And why in heaven's name you should concoct that fairy tale about Margaret and me. . .'

'I didn't! She told Oliver that she wanted to marry you, and you were always hanging round her. . .' She felt the Professor's enormous chest heave with silent amusement and went on indignantly: 'Well, you were—how was I to know? You see, you would have done very well for her—rich and living the kind of life she likes, and Oliver likes you. . .'

'He shall come and stay with us, my dearest. As I have already told you, someone must exercise those animals until our children are old enough to do it for themselves. But Dirk—Aunt Bess told you about him?—will see that Oliver has his fair share of living here. You haven't said that you will marry me, Jenny.'

Her voice was very quiet. 'I'm waiting to be asked.'

She felt his chest heave again and heard a rumble of laughter. 'Jenny soft as silk at last! Will you marry me?'

She stood on tiptoe to kiss him. 'I couldn't bear it if I didn't.' She was kissed at some length until she said: 'Eduard, just a minute—why didn't you tell me? I mean, at Solendijk—you see, it seemed as if you and Margaret. . .and yet in Alkmaar I almost. . . You did mean all those things you said in Alkmaar?'

'Oh, my dear heart, yes.'

Jenny heaved a sigh of pure happiness, and then: 'Eduard, your parents—do you suppose they'll mind? Will they like me?'

'They loved you. They couldn't understand why I hadn't snapped you up weeks ago.'

'Well, why didn't you?'

He smiled down at her, pulling her closer. 'I thought I'd told you; I'm too old and arrogant and. . .'

'Fiddlesticks,' said Jenny, 'you're exactly my idea of a perfect husband.' She kissed him to prove it. 'We'd better go and tell Aunt Bess. She will be surprised.'

They started up the staircase. 'No, she won't, my darling. I told her I was going to marry you.'

'Oh—did you? But I might not have wanted to.'

They had achieved the top of the narrow staircase by now. 'Then I should have persuaded you.'

'How?'

'Like this, my little love.' He bent his head to kiss her once more. Presently she said: 'Eduard— dear Eduard, there are a lot of questions. . .'

'Nothing that can't wait for an answer, my darling. This, on the other hand, can't wait either.'

And Jenny, kissed into silence, happily agreed.

MILLS & BOON®

BETTY NEELS

COLLECTOR'S EDITION

If you have missed any of the previously published titles in the Betty Neels Collector's Edition our Customer Care department will be happy to advise you of titles currently in stock. Alternatively send in a large stamped addressed envelope and we will be pleased to provide you with full details by post. Please send your SAE to:

Betty Neels Collector's Edition
Customer Care Department
Eton House
18-24 Paradise Road
Richmond
Surrey TW9 1SR

Customer Care Direct Line - 0181 288 2888

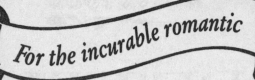

MILLS & BOON®

*B*etty Neels is a unique and much loved author and, as you will know, she often uses medical settings.

*I*f you enjoy stories with a medical flavour, featuring doctors and nurses battling to save lives and find lasting love—and peopled with characters as heartwarming as those created by Betty Neels, then look out for the Mills & Boon® series,

Medical Romance™

which features four new stories each month.

Available at most branches of WH Smith, John Menzies, Martins, Tesco, Volume One and Safeway

For the spirited lover in you...

$\mathcal{P}$resents™

Passionate, compelling, provocative romances you'll never want to end.

Eight brand new titles each month